When to Walk

REBECCA GOWERS

CANONGATE

Edinburgh · New York · Melbourne

First published in Great Britain in 2007 by
Canongate Books Ltd, 14 High Street,
Edinburgh EH1 1TE

1

British Library Cataloguing-in-Publication Data
A catalogue record for this book is available on
request from the British Library

ISBN 978 1 84195 892 7

Typeset in Berkeley Old Style by Palimpsest Book Production Ltd,
Grangemouth, Stirlingshire

Printed and bound in Great Britain by Creative Print and Design,
Ebbw Vale, Wales

www.canongate.net

1

Saturday

A few days ago I was drifting past The Admiral when a man lurched towards me with a black-and-white photocopy of a ten-pound note. As he spoke he spat. He said, 'Got a couple of fivers?'

I gestured to indicate that I hadn't and felt relieved that it was true.

At once he amended his deal to a single fiver, which I did have.

A tenner for a fiver: great.

I'd noticed him about the streets for some time, always in a filthy-looking overcoat. Close up, he smelled filthy as well, added to which his shoes were split and lacking their laces.

He repeated his new offer with escalating volume as though he thought I might be deaf. 'A tenner for a fiver,' he said. 'A bleeding tenner for a bleeding fiver.'

I am, in fact, quite deaf in one ear, but he didn't know.

Go round the corner where The Admiral is, wander along the High Street and there are five shops with photocopy machines: two newsagents, a stationery shop and two actual copy shops. In four of them a single copy costs 5p. The fifth place, Margin's, charges 7p. Why opt for 7p? I decided it was reasonable to assume that the man's black-and-white tenner had set him back 5p, or in other words, five thousandths of what he'd hoped he would get for it. I sort of paid him attention but I didn't buy his money.

As he spat I flinched, wondering, how likely was he to have tuberculosis? Spittle as infected litter, I thought—KEEP BRITAIN TIDY. At the same time I was asking myself, was there any circumstance in which a rational person might feel tempted to spend even five pence on a single-sided photocopy of a ten-pound note? I thought: suppose this rational person had an urgent need to make a list—say there was this list but nothing to write it on, and of course the rational person's memory isn't faultless. If a man were to step forwards, wishing, for five pence only, to sell a piece of paper the size of a ten-pound note with, as it happens, printed on the back, the monochromatic image of a tenner, wouldn't the paper, now, seem cheap?

I meandered along the High Street. It was a hot, hot day.

The ten-pound-note man disappeared completely from my mind until a few hours ago.

I don't know how else to put this. My husband was explaining to me that our marriage is defunct. 'It started dying,' he said, 'in my view, pretty much as soon as we tied the knot. But anyway as far as I'm concerned, honestly, for ages it's been pretty much *defunct*.'

We were in our dingy, rental kitchen. We had just had lunch. He said the word 'defunct', and I suddenly felt sick at the smell of sardines, burnt toast and orange peel.

'And by the way, before you ask,' he said, 'I take this to

cover any duty I should maybe feel to the vow, "Till death us do part". I mean I think a kind of death, that's—a kind of death, that's exactly what we're talking about.'

His mother is romantic and named him Constantine, but he's mostly known as Con. And I've mostly thought this funny if I've thought about it at all.

He began his spiel as soon as we'd finished eating: food in, words out. There we were at the table, still with our plates in front of us, orange peel, fiddly skeins of pith, water glasses. He announced that I ought to know it had been a while since he'd thought of himself as my husband.

'That's it, honestly, it's over. Game over. Three years I've really tried but I think you ought to know that it's been a while now since I've thought of myself—'

He shifted in his chair. When I ventured to glance at him he was always staring either at the sink, or a few inches above it out of the window, from which angle the view is of a wall.

'You're impossible and I don't mean to be rude but, someone who doesn't talk, it's pretty much—I don't want you to feel—I mean I've basically had enough.'

He didn't put it like this, didn't use either of the words I'm about to use, but I found he was telling me that in the person of his wife, I have degraded into an autistic vampire.

I admit though, I wasn't fully concentrating. If you think you're about to be sick it's hard to concentrate on anything else—apart, that is, from on *not* being sick.

Near the end he said, 'I'm just tired of feeling responsible for you.'

It came to me that, to Con, my life appears not unlike a black-and-white photocopy of a real life, worth, if approached in the right spirit, oh, five thousandths of the value I've been imagining for it.

I sat there gazing at my dirty plate, bewildered, shocked and guilty.

It was humid the day the ten-pound-note man tried to interest me in his deal. That evening the weather blew up into a storm, with thunder but no rain. I think the muggy heat plus his wool overcoat may explain why he smelled quite so bad. Today it's still hot, but it isn't to the same degree oppressive. Given it's meant to be autumn, the temperature must surely drop soon, and then the wind, or a snap frost, will strip a swathe of foliage off the council's spindly, street-improving lime trees.

I have no idea what I'm meant to be thinking, but I find my mind stalls on the fact that I don't earn enough to pay the rent here alone, not to mention needing also to eat. This neighbourhood may be unexalted—it *is* unexalted: a part Victorian, part post-war, dilapidated mish-mash—but it isn't as though the rents round here are the equivalent of, say, a 3p copy machine.

I would like to ask Con about the practical difficulties that arise from the death of our arrangement, but he delivered his speech, murmured his regrets and disappeared. I heard him whip down the first flight of stairs, then abruptly stop and speak to the man who rents below us. They laughed, two doors banged, and that was it.

I suppose not everyone is bewildered the day their marriage ends. I feel shocked but I find I'm not surprised. There's a moment three fifths of the way through a regulation slasher movie where the second-ranking female character, high-heeled and underclad, flees down an alleyway at night. It's a given that the music will tip the audience the wink that in one of the shaded stairwells up ahead, a man with an axe is coolly waiting to jump out and chop her to bits. When—!*bam!*—he jumps out and chops her to bits, the audience is—!*bam!*— shocked; but not, I think, surprised.

Con's spiel went on and on. It made me feel sick. I have it only in gobbets—'you're impossible', &c., 'game over', '*defunct*', 'I mean I've basically had enough'. One of his lines was to do with how my best next step would be to make my own friends.

He said something, not in these words, like, 'Make your own fucking friends.'

How am I supposed to do this? I don't know. I warm to people who read books. I like the way they sit, hunched over, deliberately deaf. To me the ideal reader looks like someone who, even on a night bus, with only a dim light overhead, and surrounded entirely by drunkards, those drunkards no doubt to include the driver, would be capable of giving off the atmosphere of an aspirant curate wondering just when it became imperative to form a moral judgement.

Con didn't say, in these words, 'Make your own fucking friends.' It was more like: 'I think you need to widen your social circle. I know this may sound feeble but I sometimes get the impression my friends prefer you to me and you can't do everything through me it's just—it's suffocating. I wish you'd get some people of your own. I wish you'd live your own life and leave mine alone. I've had it. You should get some new friends or something.'

He did also say, 'I expect there are things about *me* that *you* find difficult.' But he didn't pause for breath, and besides, all I could think of that instant was that I hate the way he insists on 100-watt light bulbs.

He used to talk to me, a lot, about music. He'd flit all over the keyboard to illustrate his points. He'd stick the words in any old how, but his playing would be near-continuous. He used to speak to me through music, with a few words in the mix.

Forget 100-watt light bulbs, it would have been something to reply to him that I find it distressing that we don't talk like this any more.

Christ but—an *autistic vampire*? When Dracula first reaches England from Transylvania, his ship puts in at Whitby. If you stand on the south cliff above the little port there, it's striking how the harbour is shaped like a diagram in cross-section of a woman's reproductive organs.

I can't think of anything else to say about vampires.

I'm only partly deaf. For example, I can make out that someone has begun clattering around in the downstairs flat, and I'm hearing this from the top floor of the building. Ours is a flat on two floors, a maisonette.

This word 'maisonette', it strikes me as being superfluous even though I just used it.

As of about a week ago, the maisonette downstairs is being rented by Mr and Mrs Shaw. At least, according to the one letter that's come for them, that's what they're called.

My best bet is that Mr Shaw had a previous wife, lost most of his money divorcing and moved in here with a newer, younger and blonder Mrs Shaw on the promise that when life improves, they'll get a place of their own.

The two of them have been shouting a lot since they arrived. A couple of days ago, when I was still functionally married myself, I said at breakfast, 'I won't be surprised if before you know it those new people downstairs have split up and disappeared again.'

Con replied, 'If they can yell at each other and get it out in the open, I should think that gives them a pretty good chance of being able to beat their problems.'

When I was small, I latched on to the notion that people traumatised by divorce go deaf, and I believed it for a long time, despite all the divorced people I knew being able to hear—not least, in time, my own parents. It's like a bad joke now to think that my own half-deafness has caught up with me at last.

I feel loudly deaf: deaf in my head somehow, not discounting the fact that through the open window I can hear the 3s and 9s round the corner on the High Street, the electric bell of the Minimart pwanging down below next door, people talking on the pavement, Mr and Mrs Shaw bashing about in their flat, even the fitful rustling of air in the lime leaves.

I suppose I've long since loosely understood that there might be a hand holding an axe in a dark stairwell up ahead waiting to leap out and chop my marriage to bits. I didn't think what we had was perfect or anything; and anyway, what would a perfect marriage be? Robert Browning considered the idea of a perfect marriage distasteful. *Perfection* was distasteful, he thought; although, now I've gone and said that, I find myself coming up with a kind of perfection I'm sure he would have liked.

Some years ago I saw a film about which I remember next to nothing, and no doubt the bit I think I remember differs from what actually happens on celluloid, but that doesn't matter. In the clip as I recall it, a young man is living in poverty in an attic in Paris. Presumably he's French. Day after day he watches for a girl, who, far below him in the street, makes the odd modest purchase at a little food shop opposite his building. She's beautiful—in the circumstances, I forgive her—and he is smitten, of course; but in trying to dream up an inoffensive way to get her to notice him, he grows ill. Minutes pass, and then one day he approaches her as she looks over the vegetables, fruits and whatever else, stacked in crates outside the shop. 'I believe you just dropped this,' he says, and holds out an egg.

I think that, like Rapunzel, or the Lady of Shalott, I could persuade myself right now this minute to suffer my way down and out of my building, ready to blow my life to bits, if I only knew that there was someone waiting in the Minimart to woo me with a perfect lie.

By a 'perfect lie', I mean an undeceitful lie, that is, in its lack of pretence, graced with a peculiar truth.

It's a question, though, whether the love-sick young Frenchman thought to cook his egg first, because, what would it be like to go sloping about the place, in fast-moving crowds, say, with an uncooked egg in one's hand, or, worse still, in

8

one's trouser pocket? Would a person not become, in such a case, even if painlessly, a kind of cripple?

I talk freely about cripples. I know what it is to be a kind of cripple, so I allow myself to talk freely about cripples; and I don't by this mean the deafness in one of my ears.

I've just watched a four-pigeon pigeon fight. I spend a hopeless amount of time observing the bumbly, cack-toed, mostly failed pigeons that pace the sills and ledges of the minicab office opposite. Lots of pigeons are cripples.

I'm not working, I'm watching pigeon fights, &c. I should be writing a piece for work. I have a deadline at the end of the week. But my marriage collapsed at lunch time, and, although I'm sitting here and could be working, as regards work, I seem to be taking the afternoon off. Inside myself I'm not thinking anything much other than: he's gone. *He's gone.* I don't know where, but, unsurprisingly—sort of unsurprisingly, shockingly—anyway, *out of the blue*, he's gone. He's disappeared. *He's gone.* I wasn't good enough. *He's gone*, &c. &c.

As for Con's line, 'I wish you'd live your own life and leave mine alone'—I feel compelled to mention that at another point in his spiel, he accused me of living entirely inside my own head, and at yet another, of not living any sort of life at all. I think these comments contributed to my remembering the man outside The Admiral with his photocopied ten-pound note.

Con said: 'You have difficulties, I know. I know. I'm not saying you don't. But it isn't a reason to give up. I'm not saying anything, but plenty of people have worse problems than you.'

*

The racket downstairs is hard to interpret. It could almost be that the Shaws are dragging their furniture around. Why do that, though?

For something like a year, Bobbo Stothard lived in that flat. She left three weeks ago to join her elderly sister in Glasgow. Bobbo led me to understand that the ground floor of this building was going to be treated for damp. I therefore wasn't expecting it when replacement tenants moved in.

I liked Bobbo, but she disconcerted me, so I tried to keep out of her way. She belonged to an outfit called the Churches' Circle of Psychical and Spiritual Studies. She had an enormous reserve of anecdotes about other people's encounters with benevolent ghosts, which was fine by me, until—inevitably, I felt afterwards—she one day said, 'I don't talk about it, but I'm a sensitive.' I couldn't bring myself to ask her to elaborate.

The best story she ever told me was not a CCPSS one. It was a moral fable about an event in the life of her governess, Mme Genet. Mme Genet, though Swiss, had been caught up as a child in the Russian revolution. The night at last came when her mother decided that they must escape Moscow. The weather was bitter, the two of them had no food and the political situation was getting worse and worse. They went to bid farewell to a friend, who pressed them to take a bag with a few crusts in it. As little Genet and her mother slunk along the darkened streets, they passed a man leaning against an iron fence, holding forth a cupped hand. Genet's mother said they must give him one of the crusts. Genet protested. How would they ever escape Moscow if they started to give away their food before they'd even begun? Her mother put a crust in the man's hand. The crust fell to the ground because he was dead.

10

Saturday

I don't know what I meant when I said that this was a moral fable.

~

Just now I went and lay on the bed and then got up again and came back here. This is a story about Bobbo. The day she was due to leave, and did leave, I made my way downstairs and knocked on her door. 'I'm so sorry I haven't helped,' I said. 'Can I help?'

'You *are* sweet,' she replied, 'but my friends have all rallied and look—see,' she gestured behind her, 'I'm fully packed up, raring to go. But step inside, why don't you? I have some special soaps going begging. I couldn't fit them in. You take them for me.'

I was touched by this, in part because it was so obviously untrue that she would have packed everything she owned save a few bars of soap. She went to fetch them. I didn't step inside.

Their cloying smell caught me off guard. There were three of them, each wrapped in tissue paper with a paper bracelet gummed on top, the bracelets printed with complex coats of arms. I held my awkward haul in my hands and read off to myself, PARFUMEURS DEPUIS 1841. Bobbo herself repeated a word that sounded something like '*Blomchet*', not written anywhere I could see. I was, as I say, touched. I like the 1840s above any other decade.

'If you don't use them straight away,' she said, 'you can keep them in your undies drawer. Scents them, as it were.' There was a hint of pleasure to the way she added, 'A handy old trick.'

I found myself wondering why Bobbo of all people would

think to perfume her knickers, and at once a fact came into my mind, though I doubt it's really true, that Japanese men, *in industrial numbers*—this vivid phrase also just came to me—like to buy what they believe to be the slightly soiled knickers of adolescent girls, having coin-op machines that dispense them in purpose-made containers, along with condoms, cigarettes or whatever. Without thinking about it, I sighed, causing Bobbo, I saw peripherally, to shrink, as though she took it I had judged her foolish, which indeed, unjustly, I rather had.

So Bobbo left. And now Con has disappeared, *he's gone*, &c. I'm not persuaded the Shaws will last either. When they yell at each other downstairs their words are too muffled to decipher, but the general sound strikes me as harsh and cheerless, not, what?—robustly constructive?

The first time I saw Mr Shaw, he was sitting on the low wall outside our building eating an ice cream. He went about this with the air of someone trying to revivify a frozen breast; that was my impression, and it was so strong I didn't notice much else about him, though I did observe him well enough that he became a recognisable person to me. At the time, I wasn't aware that he had moved in downstairs.

I saw Mr Shaw with his ice cream, and I propped up their one letter against the hall wall the other morning—if they *are* Mr and Mrs Shaw—when I was stepping out, like the Parisian girl in the film, to make a modest purchase at the Minimart. I have also twice now passed them going in and out at the front door, not that I think I'd be able to identify Mrs Shaw in a police line-up. She stared at me and I couldn't really look back.

That's it. The pair of them haven't seemed remotely friendly during the week of our joint residence here. I suppose neither have I. Another of the reasons Con gave for leaving me was, 'You don't know how to relate to other people.'

It's one thing facts that aren't true, Japanese used-knicker vending machines and so on, but I can state for certain that at some point in the early 1840s, when she was still a child, Christina Rossetti was taken to Madame Tussaud's on a treat that was a total failure. Why? Because she'd been taught that it's rude to stare.

I can only imagine what she'd have thought of having to peer through one-way glass at a police line-up of bogus degenerates. I greatly dislike looking at people I don't know, if they are also looking at me.

It's Saturday. It's hot. I'm supposed to be working. My husband has left me. I haven't got money for the rent. The people downstairs are making a lot of noise. The pigeons can't sit still. I don't want to be thinking, *he's gone*, he's gone, *he's left me*, he's gone—but that's what I keep thinking.

I suppose I could get myself downstairs and buy a paper or something, but I don't want to do that, and besides, if I were to leave the building, I ought to visit my grandmother, Stella Ramble. I go once a week, on Saturdays. Today would be the day.

If ever I repeat the rudest joke bar none in Stella Ramble's one-time repertoire of jokes, I do so in the service of providing historical perspective on humour. Why would a woman in her nineties hate the name Stella? This isn't the joke. Because Stella is the name you give a carthorse when it has a star-shaped blaze on its forehead. That's how old she is: old enough to be troubled by the incidentals of a culture dependent on cart-horses.

I don't like horses. It could be argued that they aren't aware of themselves, but I think they understand very well indeed what they're up to.

What would it be like to fall over underneath a carthorse? More than having an uncooked egg in a trouser pocket, how this would sharpen one's senses: the mild worry about being soaked in a gallon of horse piss; the desperate fear of having your head trampled to a pulp; the smell of the creature so strong and so animal; the uncertainty as to whether an attempt to get out from under it might not provoke an attack you would otherwise have avoided; the horrible thought that it might lie down and suffocate you or fatally fracture your ribs; and all the time the ring and clatter of iron shoes on cobble stones, as the beast, too, grows nervous.

Stella Ramble's worst joke was this: 'One skin, two skin, three skin—oh dear me!' It came coupled with a teetering, concessive laugh.

She didn't confide it to me. She whispered it, at a family gathering some years ago, to my father, Middleton Ramble. She had forced him to promise that he would absolutely never repeat it, but Middleton Ramble didn't scruple to deceive his elderly mother over whether or not he would keep to himself what she'd billed as the rudest joke in the world.

While my grandmother whispered to my father, and let fly with her social laugh, I was at the far end of the table having a chat with Gander Ramble. To be strict, he isn't genuinely a Ramble. He married a great-aunt of mine, now dead, and I give him my family name because I'm fond of him.

Saturday

It is said on my side of the family that Gander Ramble is related somehow to the fiend who, in a misconceived attempt to get them clean, had the outer patina scoured off the Elgin Marbles. One day, afflicted with a curious sense of shame, I went to the British Museum to look at the result. They're superb.

Gander Ramble, the essence of well-to-do, said to me at the party in question, 'It's unsettling to find oneself the grandfather of a young man who has spent all his working days flat on his back at a garage tinkering with the undersides of cars.'

I was intrigued by this view of things. I wasn't sure I'd ever met the boy, who is, to me, no more than one of several second cousins living in Suffolk. 'I don't know,' I said after a while, 'I suppose a hundred years ago, with a little string-pulling, he could have been tucked into a perfectly respectable job in the city?'

Gander Ramble frowned. 'Gosh no, I don't think so,' he said. Then he added a remark that we both laughed over a lot, though in different registers. 'I rather think that a hundred years ago, he would have spent his working days flat on his back tinkering with the undersides of horses.'

Yes, well.

Stella Ramble likes to assert that she's unshockable. It's an oddly popular stance these days, but I don't believe her.

All the same, given she suffers from dementia and has reached the stage where she has very little short-term memory, it does sometimes cross my mind that I could, without repercussions, put her to the test. For example, I think she might minimally raise an eyebrow at the mysterious story of one of my mother's friends, and the evening gloves she rarely wore. One day this lady, gently genteel, was invited to the opera, the first invitation of its kind she had received since the death of her husband. She decided to accept, and for once to wear her special gloves. But when she fished them out from the back of the drawer, she found, to her horror, carefully deposited in all ten fingertips, a desiccated ration of shit.

To say the word 'shit' to my grandmother on the thought that she wouldn't remember two minutes later doesn't seem to me excusable.

When she was still herself, Stella Ramble held the reverse position to the one she holds now. She was mortifyingly ready to be shocked. She thought all sorts of things were 'frightfully off', such as owning folding furniture, of any description, even card tables. Items of this nature, she believed, conveyed to the world that one lived without due ease.

At a quick mental inventory, almost every stick of furniture belonging to or used by me and Con either dismantles effortlessly or folds. The very flooring in this place can be taken to bits, as we discovered soon after we moved in, when I spilled lamp oil in the main room downstairs. We got scared about our rental deposit and somehow worked out that we could knife up the stained carpet tile and exchange it for a clean one lifted out from under the non-fire-regulation sofa.

Over time there have been more spills, of candle wax, coffee and the like, and we don't now think twice about swapping the tiles around. A stranger walking in would find that the main room floor, which is of an unnameable dark hue, looks, though mottled, acceptably uniform across its visible expanse. But if that person only knew to check, the sofa floats above a hidden terrain of mismanagement, filth and deceit.

*

Saturday

I dare say Stella Ramble's joke would disappoint even someone capable of recognising that its entertainment value these days lies solely in how unfunny it is. The concept of lack-of-funniness being occasionally in itself amusing isn't all that outré, but there are perhaps those who would need head exercises to get it.

Further back even than Stella Ramble's far-away youth, there maunders a great supply of Robert Browning jokes:

> 'In the Hub.' Hub Mother (shouting downstairs) — Minerva, are you going to bed? Hub Daughter — Let me have another half hour with Robert, ma. Hub Mother — Another half hour with Robert. Goodness gracious! Have you a man in the house! Hub Daughter — The idea! I'm reading Browning.

This joke also, correctly interpreted, is informatively unfunny, providing a contrast with 'Rules for Reading Browning', from an 1890 issue of the *Boston Globe*, which derives any humour it might have now from the fear that it *wasn't* intended to be amusing:

> You must absorb him through the pores of your soul. Make yourself a sponge, hurl yourself at Browning and soak. Sit down and read a poem whole. Do not try to understand. Do not stop to query in your reading, "What does this mean?" Never mind: read on. Plunge through it in any way, simply calling the words; then re-plunge and re-re-plunge. And, then, when you have re-re-plunged for a considerable length of time, varying from hours to months, according to the perspicacity of your intellect, you begin to see the parts of the poem, the whole in relation to the parts, and the parts in relation to each other.

I know: what kind of maniac collects Robert Browning jokes? I have this compelling sense that when at last I find the right one, I'll understand what the point is.

The pigeons opposite—I worry that one of them is going to end up paralysed on the pavement. It's as though something purposeful is happening over there: gang warfare! insurrection! unarmed revolt!

I'm not sure there has ever been much point to Stella Ramble, but when she still had opinions there was a great deal she was down on. Along with folding furniture, pastels, the Jews and partial nudity, she was more than sniffy about suicides. I need hardly add that, in her readiness to be offended, she was nerve-wrackingly offensive herself.

I suspect, however, that she didn't think her opinions through. I imagine it's more the case that, as a matter of instinct, she reflected back whatever she felt would please those men of her own class upon whom she depended, her long list of dislikes providing, in effect, a glimpse into the soul of the casually superior English gent.

What I'm saying is that her moral gaze was a filmy sort of moonshine.

Forget my work deadline, I should have fitted in visiting her this afternoon, but my marriage folded, and when Con left I just went and lay down. Then I came upstairs to work, which I am not doing, though I sit and write, nevertheless:

A few days ago I was drifting past The Admiral when a man lurched towards me with a black-and-white photocopy of a ten-pound note. As he spoke he spat. He said, 'Got a couple of fivers?'

I gestured to indicate that I hadn't and felt relieved that it was true.

Here I sit writing—yes—and now it's twilight, and I can smell the heat being given up by the paving stones, tarmac, concrete, brickwork and litter of my street. Evening is in the air, and here I sit.

My mind has repeatedly fallen, all these hours, into a deadening loop: *He's gone.* 'It's over.' *He's left me.* 'Game over. Three years, I've really tried, but—'

At the conclusion of Con's spiel, which was, of course, longer by a long chalk than the speech he gave at our wedding—after he left the flat, after he laughed on the stairs with Mr Shaw and the two doors banged—I stepped through from the kitchen into the main room and went and lay down on the sofa.

What else is there to say except that Stella Ramble, in the old days, would have been unimpressed by the sofa. If you feel like it, you can split it into three easy-chairs, two of them with a single arm, and the third with none.

There was the sofa and I lay down. A few hours passed and I got up again, came up here, started to write, and now I'm exhausted. It's painful for me to sit still for long stretches. At first I lay down for a while. Since then I've been up here sitting.

If I could face it, I would slip out and join the drunkards at The Admiral. Perhaps the ten-pound-note man is in there this minute debating with the landlord, George, the question of whether or not you can pay for a pint with photocopied money.

I'm fairly sure all we have by way of drink in this miserable maisonette is a single bottle of beer. I intend, shortly, to go down-stairs to our laminated rental kitchen, to sit on one of the unstable chairs at the pull-out table and to drink that bottle of beer.

I have friends, I do have friends, *my own fucking friends* I find myself hoping, Beata and Johnson specially, but not only Beata and Johnson, also Pat and Charlie, for example, who are both in the States right now. I also have some family, as who doesn't?

I haven't called anybody because I've never really brought up with anyone about marriage seeming so hard. Plus, I'm worried Con might come back. I'm worried Con will come back, and will tell me his whole spiel was a sort of mistake, and that we should start again, 'make a go of things'—remarks of this kind.

My plan is to give it a week. If I still have no sense of where he is after a week, perhaps then I'll call someone.

That's what I decided while I lay stagnant in the early after-noon above the fouled carpet tiles, on the non-fire-regulation, three-chairs-in-one-sofa sofa.

It's noticeable, and annoying I think, how standard crime films so often provide a victim who is lacking all the many ties that bind a normal human being. When the first vicious steps are taken by the movie's psychopath, does the beautiful heroine—or pathetic cripple heroine—call mother, brother, aunt, confidante, neighbour? Does she call the front-desk liaison officer at the nearest police station? She doesn't. She climbs up into her expensive attic and waits there to be murdered.

About Con, I can say this. I agree with him that there was some-thing wrong from the start. He proposed to me on his knees, and as he did so, I found myself anxiously wishing above any other thought that he had remained on his feet. I didn't know where to look. I'd have liked to look down, but he was down looking up, so I couldn't, as a result of which, I was left with the panicked feeling that he had missed the point of his proposal.

Con is impulsive. The scene I'm describing took place when he and I had known each other eleven days. It really was the start. We were in a park in cold weather beside an empty bandstand.

I doubt he would have proposed to me if there *had* been music, a brass band or something. Con works on film scores as an orchestrator. He earns his share of our rent, bread and orange peel—the majority share—by helping slant background music to heighten given scenes. Had there been a band that chilly day in the park, some half-cock, out-of-tune military band, perhaps the two of us wouldn't have wound up married.

The minicabs are busy. The pigeons just flew off. The green has drained from the lime trees; they're sodium-vapour grey. People in the street are calling out to each other making plans for the night. How long ago did I think I was about to drink the beer? It's getting late and my bones ache, but at the prospect of a beer I suppose I can shift myself down one floor. I've sat here for ages whittling the hours. Perhaps at last the hours will consent to whittle me, &c.

~

Oh, wow! Seconds after I'd decided to go downstairs anyway there was a loud banging on the door to the flat. I assumed—

I didn't stop to consider anything else—that Con had come home again, and that, although he'd made it into the building, he had somehow lost the key to our place and was banging on the door. Hateful to say, I felt a rush of relief. I got to my feet and, as far as I'm able to, hurried on down to let him in. The banging didn't stop as I hobbled down the stairs, and when I opened the door: wow! There stood Mrs Shaw in an incredible bad temper smelling densely of cigarettes.

The earliest citation in the *OED* for 'wow' dates to 1513: 'Out on thir wanderand spiritis, wow! thow cryis.'

What Mrs Shaw cried was, 'Fucking shitting bastard.' Though her voice was extremely loud, she seemed to be communicating with herself. I noticed obliquely that she's older than I'd thought, by some years older than me. She looked thirty-three? Thirty-three? Maybe thirty-four.

I don't know why I spoke at all, but I said, 'Your husband?'

'My husband?' she growled.

'Oh,' I said.

'Not my husband,' she said. 'Not my husband. Your fucking git of a bastard husband.'

I stepped backwards. When people shout it makes me notice my deafness in a more particular, more unpleasant way.

She clicked past me—she was wearing glinting red high-heels—off the landing lino and onto our carpet tiles. She threw herself down on the sofa. 'I'm not fucking waiting in till one of them gets back,' she said. 'Lock the fucking door. If you've got any blankets, I don't want pneumonia. I've had it up to here. I've truly fucking had it.' She sighed and added, 'What a fucking amateur,' before mumbling, 'All I ever wanted was to be a counter clerk.'

I stood there, thrown, until it came to me that by 'counter', she meant the solid object.

I obediently followed her instructions and bolted the door—against which of our husbands, I still have no idea—then came back upstairs and fetched the lurid pink blanket given to us by Con's mother. When I got downstairs again I had to lay it over Mrs Shaw myself because she'd already closed her eyes. I could tell from her clotted breathing that she was asleep. She'd fallen asleep in two minutes. I sort of flipped the blanket across her. She had her head on a sea-green velvet cushion that I took from Stella Ramble's house. The effect, with her bright blond hair, was beautiful. She, I found, was beautiful—or you might say pretty; worn but pretty—smart even, in a way.

After I'd done the blanket, I went through into the kitchen. It has top-grade, chequer-pattern lino tiles, the best floor in the building. I try to avoid stepping on the pale squares, for no good reason whatsoever. I fetched the beer out of the fridge and came back upstairs again.

Not for the first time today, I feel sick.

I didn't ask her what she meant by 'Your fucking git of a bastard husband', because I didn't want to encourage her shouting, besides which, when she was in the act of saying it, I somehow thought she must be making a mistake.

The word 'amateur', peculiarly, is worse. Amateur what? If she weren't asleep, I might almost ask her that: *Amateur what?*

Now that I'm up here sitting again, I'm no longer tired.

*

I feel unnerved by the thought that Mrs Shaw may shout at me some more in the morning. She made the walls ring. The ten-pound-note man shouted at me, and Mrs Shaw just shouted at me, before which, I'm fairly certain I haven't been shouted at since school.

I wouldn't choose to sleep in our bed tonight if the sofa were free. It's hard to believe that my marriage has ended. Anyway, it turns out the sofa isn't free, so I'm going to go to bed, not that I'm tired, although I am exhausted. There isn't much else to do and I have to work tomorrow, and Con may come home in the morning, I don't know.

I meant, just now, to go to bed. But as I wrote, *and Con may come home in the morning, I don't know*, a stultifying weariness crept over me and pinioned me.

For a while I remained here, absolutely still.

Then, after a while, unable to stop myself, I read through everything I've written today: *Rapunzel, Dracula*; 'A tenner for a fiver'; *'defunct'*—wow. Since when? I find myself wondering. 'Make your own fucking friends.' *I warm to people who read books.*

Hey, I think perhaps you dropped this egg.

2

Sunday

Whenever it was I went to bed, I didn't fall asleep until about three a.m., and I woke again bluntly, overwhelmed at being alone. These past hours I have experienced flickers of an almost detached interest in my freedom, but more of the time—most of it since Con left—I've been juddering round the thought that first there is this limbo, then, Christ, the bureaucratic—the enormity is defeating. Divorce, paper termination and—then?

To begin with I didn't remember about Mrs Shaw.

I was still in bed gazing at the ceiling when it came to me that she was a small added reason for the world's feeling ominous. I listened out for her but didn't hear anything. All I could hear was buses and cars and the Minimart bell, and birds, and the sound made by a delivery lorry reversing.

The room heated up with the rising of the sun, which came to shine right in through the window. For a couple of hours I just lay there in a flop, though my mind skittered.

I said to myself: imagine you're sitting outside a café reading a book, and a waiter comes over with the cup of coffee you ordered at the bar. Imagine you're annoyed to find, first sip, that it's barely even tepid, but that as this allows you to take a large swallow straight away, you do. If, as you do, a man runs out from inside the café, stares at your cup, a ghastly look crosses his face and he shouts at you that you've drunk poison and have only thirty seconds to live, assuming you believe him—what next?

I decided I would probably scribble something in the margin of the book in front of me, except my biro wasn't working the last time I tried to use it and where's my pencil?

For those thirty seconds, what? I suspected I would be passive and yet violently alert.

Not merely this morning, but the whole time since Con left yesterday I've felt a sickening passive alertness. As I sit here, I find one bottle of beer and about three hours' sleep haven't done much to alleviate this. The pressure of my circumstances is beginning to do something unpleasant to me.

If I were a man, I would say that I've been unmanned. As I'm not, this looks like a bad pun; though the stupid truth is, I woke up and just lay in bed for a couple of hours, violently alert but unmanned.

When I did limp my way through the main room to the kitchen, Mrs Shaw wasn't there. It was a let-down to find nothing but the folded-up pink blanket. I suppose she's back in her own flat. I haven't heard any yelling.

Con's remark about the Shaws shouting at each other, 'I should think that gives them a pretty good chance of being able to beat their problems'—it's tempting to read this as a sideways comment on our own set-up; but it strikes me that enough people do get by on talk alone, with no raised voices.

Anyway, I think it isn't words, at whatever pitch and volume, that have killed my marriage, so much as other languages that Con and I appear not to have in common.

This suggestion would doubtless cause a healthy mind to leap to what was once called 'the language of the bedchamber', but I have to say, sex didn't feature in the list of Con's reproaches.

It happens that sexual intimacy is, itself, an archaic meaning of the word 'conversation', hence 'conjugal conversation'—sex within marriage—or the old legal term for the adulterous pleasures of married women, 'criminal conversation'. In fact—sadly, one might venture, as it seems not to reflect well on conjugal sex—it was in this latter phrase, shortened in nineteenth-century press reports on divorces to 'crim. con.', that the usage survived longest.

Whatever else, and this I did discuss with my husband—and I realise as I sit here that we had more or less a party line on it—whatever else, however poorly we managed other sorts of talking, our bodies some time since hit upon a conversation that we agreed was fierce and ludicrous enough to suit us both.

In his spiel, Con said, 'Probably most people's problems begin in bed, I guess, but, fuck knows how, I'd say that for us sex has probably kept us glued together much longer than we would have otherwise, despite the unstraightforward,' he smiled, faintly, 'the complicated—I don't know, perhaps because of it, you know?'

Of course, I'm wondering about this now, I mean about the party line, that for us this particular conversation worked. The person you're married to disappears on you, surely anyone would wonder?

*

27

When at last I got out of bed this morning, I said to myself that I must now think about something other than splitting up, being left, *he's gone*, &c. But it isn't possible to enforce a decision of this kind. I seem condemned to brood on the subject.

So I limped downstairs. I was disappointed Mrs Shaw wasn't there. I had felt curious to catch another look at her asleep, seeing that we've sort of spoken now. After I'd made myself a cup of coffee, I came back up to the bedroom, sat down here at my table and started dividing divorces into types.

First, there was the divorce that arises when the people in question come to know each other too well and don't like what they find. Second, there was the opposite problem, where one person in a marriage grows to resent the impossibility of ever fully knowing the other, or being known by the other, in the manner sought. Taking these as two basic forms of failure, had my own marriage not disintegrated under the strain of the second?

Con said to me, 'You're borderline anti-social.' This sounds like something out of a textbook, but what does he know? 'If you're going to be so absurdly disconnected from the world,' he said, 'don't delude yourself you aren't also disconnected from me. It's a pain, frankly, having to work out what's going on in your head.' I believe what he really meant by this was that he wishes I understood *him* in a different way.

Why? Well, the most trenchant reason he gave me yesterday for describing our marriage as dead had nothing to do with sex, vampires, speechlessness or any of these things. It was the fact that I hate music. 'Anyway,' he said, 'how can I be expected to live with someone who hates music?'

Sunday

Yesterday, I thought: how can you propose divorce to someone because they hate music? Today I'm thinking: if you found you were married to someone who hated music, how could you not divorce them?

As to whether his accusation is true, naturally things aren't that simple.

I don't want to go on about Con, but am inclined briefly to mention that at least in his job he's a complete parasite himself. After all, what is an orchestrator? Day after day he slogs his aestheticised guts out for what might be classed a film music factory.

When Con first fell for me, I think it was partly because I'm the child of a musician. My father in his heyday was a professional pianist, though his performing career was cut short by arthritis. I was expected to understand, as an insider, Con's dream of composing great works; yet once we were married he began to make such remarks as, 'You don't get your father. You just don't get. For a start you're deaf, but that doesn't even matter, you have no clue what's going on with the man.'

Con understood my father; I didn't. I never objected out loud to this line of attack. Well, what did Con really mean? I have become accomplished at letting these assaults drift out of my mind.

I don't in principle mourn the way that words can shrivel, but I do regret what has happened to the offing. The 'offing', in its original meaning, was the outermost edge of the sea you could see. Now that we English have generally got over our nautical past, the term has faded into metaphor. Talk of something being 'in the offing', and you don't think of Dracula's salt-soaked vessel as spotted on the horizon from the cliffs above Whitby, you think, for example, of a formal divorce that's a bit of a way away but coming towards you. And why always towards? I don't know.

When Con makes assertions that feel unthinkable, I let them drift to the offing on an outwards tide. For a while they may bob about at the edge, but soon enough they tip over into a greater vagueness beyond.

~

What was I on about earlier? I'm bored by how frightened my thoughts are.

Imagine you're sitting outside a café reading a book, and a waiter comes over with the cup of coffee you ordered at the bar.

I guess I woke up and worried about the mechanics of death-by-poisoned-coffee because some part of my mind was remembering that I had a date with Johnson Pike mid-morning at The Hole in the Wall. I've known Johnson since I was twelve. He unquestionably qualifies as *my own fucking friend*. He meets me away from the flat because he doesn't like the flat, but he treks over to my high street to save me trekking the distance to his.

Johnson has artistic thoughts. His great ploy of the moment is to organise an Exhibition of Temperatures. I want to say to him, why not just direct people to a sauna, or a botanical gardens' glass house? But somehow there's more to it than this, to do with mirrors and lights and I don't know what. When he talks about it, I can't make myself concentrate. I enjoy the sound of him being passionate about his projects, but I don't care much what they are. He complains at intervals that nobody takes him seriously, and I'm sympathetic for the very reason that I don't take him seriously myself. In this way I am not such a good friend.

I rarely forget an engagement, and never one with Johnson, but I forgot about coffee at The Hole in the Wall. When the telephone went my stomach contracted, my hands shook, and for the first time in ages I lifted the phone to my deaf ear.

'Listen, Ramble,'—I switched sides—'rear end down here this minute: I'm about to be propositioned by a bloke in baby-blue cowboy boots.' In a desperate voice, he added, 'Run!', which he doubtless considered a joke.

'Sorry, sorry, sorry,' I said, sliding along the thinly padded seat on the wall side of Johnson's table. 'My mistake. I don't know what happened.'

He gave me an odd, penetrating look.

I had been assuming, somewhere in all my fluster, that Johnson would lift my spirits—I bit my lip—just by being himself, that he would steady me without trying; but our exchange, such as it was, had the reverse effect, so that I now found myself sitting there feeling duplicitous and prickly.

'What is it?' he said.

'Nothing.'

There was another frisson between us. I wanted to apologise and leave. Effortfully I said, 'Yuki Matsuri something something. Your kind of thing maybe. Japanese illuminated ice sculptures.' I was talking about my work.

A woman came in and let the door slam behind her. She wore a clingy top in broad tiger print. Her bra, where it bit into

her, was graphically apparent underneath. She slopped down at
the next table and picked up the photocopied menu of TODAY'S
SPECIALS, 'Ice Cream Sunday' included. Perhaps they meant this,
today being a Sunday. She didn't closely read the piece of paper.

Johnson made some sort of private calculation, then leant
towards me and lowered his voice. 'It's daft, isn't it,' he
murmured, 'how people wear leopard or snake prints or whatever in order to make themselves look like dangerous animals,
when the animals themselves are kitted up like that so they
come off like heaps of old stones or dust, or dead grass. I
mean what people are *really* dressing up like isn't snakes and
tigers, it's dried out scrubland or swamp mud.'

'Or like snow,' I said, 'as in, as in arctic rabbits. I mean *ermine*.'

'Hey listen, don't keep giving me all this ice shit,' he said.
'Here we are, blissful Indian summer. Let's talk about the
sunshine while we still can. As my mate Evan says, "Sufficient
unto the day the weather thereof."'

Another woman came in and sat down opposite the first.

'God!' she said.

'I know.'

'How's tricks?'

'Me?' said the first woman.

'I don't know, how's the kids?' said the second.

'They're all right. They're kids aren't they? I worry about
them twentyfour-seven, but I know they're okay really.'

Johnson raised his eyes to the ceiling.

'So, he paying anything? You got any dosh off him yet?
Right, sorry. Ask a stupid question.'

'As if, right.'

'Does he ever ring them or what's he like about that?'

'When I hear his voice on the phone,' said the first woman listlessly, 'I want to chuck it.'

The waitress with red hair—I know them all, I recognise them in the aisles of the Minimart—came over and took orders for teas and coffees from both tables.

Johnson stared at me. 'You look peaky,' he said.

I replied, *'Thinking of getting away in the spring?'*

This is the first line of the article I'm supposed to be working on. In a removed part of myself, I thought: if I were to tell Johnson that Con has left me, he'd say something along the lines of, 'Darling, personally speaking I hoped you'd divorce him the instant you told me he was a fan of that creep, Virginia Woolf.'

'Because the thing is,' said the first woman, 'you know, you don't want anyone to take them away from you, so you don't feel you can complain, but it's just so much bloody work, you know, and I can't afford to go out, and, bloody shoes, they cost the same for kids they do for grown-ups. Billy wakes up at six every morning and I want to hit him, and then I'm worrying, how's he going to grow up right without a dad? But when he does call them I just want to smack someone, like— I mean I don't, but I feel like it.'

'It's too soon,' said the second woman. 'You can't say yet, you have to get used to it.'

'I can't stop worrying about them twentyfour-seven,' said the first woman. 'I don't even know if they're going to grow up normal.'

'For God's sake,' whispered Johnson, 'what could be more normal?'

Anxiously, I tried to distract him. 'So, what's the story?'

Johnson always asks, 'So what's the story?'

He grinned. 'You know the fashion for jade in the twenties?'

'No I mean what's the story with you?'

'Darling, patience!' he said. 'I've just received my first ever inheritance: a disgusting portrait, "after Kneller", of a certain, blighted Mrs Amberley, and a theoretically jade bead necklace that will be worth hundreds of pounds if it doesn't happen to be glass, which I'm sure it will.'

'Oh. An inheritance from—?'

'Did you know I had an elderly relative called Cinderella?'

'Seriously?'

'How's your lunatic Granny by the way?'

'Oh no don't. Tell me about Cinderella,' I said.

'Okay, well, one of my great-, wait—great-*great*-uncles, up Dad's maternal line, was Governor of Uganda way back when, colonial oppressor blah blah blah 1920s, and he had a wife who was a depressive so he sent her home and took up instead with his girl secretary, who he eventually married after the wife died, but, before that the secretary acted as his wife in all but name, and everyone in Africa knew about it and was fine about it except when it came to official balls pardon my blah blah blah, which she wasn't allowed to attend, leading her to be known across the continent as *Cinderella*, which stayed with her the whole of the rest of her life even after they did marry. Well, amazingly, she's only just died—he died years ago—and there never were any children so she left the necklace and the picture to what she described as my father's "children", all of which happen to be me.'

'Phoo,' I said. My mind was taking in the details like one of those old departures boards in a railway station where all the little flaps fall over in a torrent. 'So, well, I mean, what—?'

I lost my way and had to start again. 'If it's genuine, will you wear this necklace? What will you do with it?'

'I hardly think so.' Johnson stared meditatively at the café's advertising board outside on the baking pavement: POP IN FOR A LIGHT SNACK TREAT YOURSELF UNBEATABLE VALUE. In a small voice he said, 'I'll sell it and buy myself a diamond butt plug.'

I felt admonished.

As I mooched home I asked myself why I was mooching home, and whether the word 'home' properly described any longer the place where I happen to live. Though I let myself in as quietly as possible, I walked in my usual way down the hall, and after I'd passed the lower flat door, Mrs Shaw stuck her head out. It's silly to be calling her this, she can't be that much older than me, although for some reason I think of her as grown up in a way that I'm not—anyway, I have no other name for her and I'm getting used to *Mrs Shaw*.

'Take you round The Admiral tonight?' she said.

I turned just slightly.

'I owe you one. Know you like a beer.' This latter observation was tinged with what sounded like defiance.

I couldn't think of a response other than, 'I thought you were asleep.'

'You thought wrong,' she said.

To this, I couldn't formulate any reply at all. I stood before her, replyless. Had she really been awake when I'd put the blanket over her?

'You took me in last night,' she said. 'You give me somewhere to kip. Others would've said no.'

'That's quite all right,' I mumbled, addressing the lino. She had on tan-coloured high-heeled sandals with pale grey leather flowers attached near the front. One or two had a pearl at the centre. The rest had trailing threads where the pearls had come off. Because the silence went on and on, I found myself adding, 'Any time.'

I don't like going to the pub with strangers. I can't hear much against the music, multiplied talking and so on, meaning that I'm forced to lip-read; but most pubs are dark, so it's not that easy to see; and with a stranger, you're forced to look the whole time at someone you don't want to look at at all; and your problems are only exacerbated if either of you gets drunk.

I jumbled too quickly up the stairs. I didn't know whether I had accepted her invitation or not but pathetically hoped I hadn't.

When I got in the answer machine was blipping with a message. The stairwell here never warms up, but the flat smelled hot, giving a touch of life to the place that it would otherwise have lacked—plus I knew there was a message. Coming in from outside, I could detect the faint odour of yesterday's orange peel. The pink blanket was still where Mrs Shaw had left it, folded on the sofa; and a few of the carpet tiles, which one would hardly think could have taken more mottling, were strewn with dots made by sunlight hitting the dirt on the window panes.

I moved around slowly. It was some time before I pressed PLAY. I tried to imagine Con's voice, but could think of nothing he might say to me, and anyway it turned out to be my 'lunatic Granny', as Johnson called her.

'Darling?' she wavered. 'Are you there? What is it? Lots of love, Stella.'

Sunday

I skipped my visit yesterday. I didn't forget, I skipped it. If you interrupt the rhythm of a mad old lady's life, this only makes her madder.

Stella Ramble went very screwy after I first put her into, as they say, *care*. The first birthday she had on the inside, she ate the candles instead of the cake. Since then, happily, she has just about reverted to the cake.

There's one quip she still comes out with that makes me feel tightly fond of her. Every week I take her a box of chocolates, and after a while she'll say, 'Goodness, look, chocolates, would you like one?' I get off the bed—there's only one chair in her room—take a couple of steps forwards—she'll often then ask what's wrong with my legs, 'Darling, what are these dodgy pins?'—and as I'm helping myself, she'll say, 'Take two. Save yourself a journey.'

I don't know why this expression has stuck with her when most of her mind is gone.

Of course, after I had her settled I was curious to know what I would find in her house, and what it might tell me about her that she herself no longer could. The job of clearing the place fell to me and took a couple of months. Right in the first week, amid all the clutter, in a drawer stuffed with French chalk, kapok, curved upholstery needles, Mecanorma Graphoplex, artificial waterflower wondershells &c., I discovered an envelope containing a small photograph of a Jewish hat shop. The way I was sorting through her junk, there was already no space on the floor. I sat down on a pile of old Sotheby's catalogues.

No one had written on the back of the picture, but there were more than enough words in the image itself. I stared at the two figures. They were strikingly contrasted. Both had taken possession of a recess, but the uniformed man, blind on purpose to the street around him, stared out of his into the military middle distance, while the boy played emperor's new clothes and looked directly at the camera. By extension, he was looking out into the future of the photograph itself. And yet how much could either of these figures have known about what was looming ahead?

I followed up on the Nazi boycott posters. It appeared that they had first been used, in a manner that this picture typifies, in 1933. I took the photograph into the home to show Stella Ramble—*Germans defend yourselves against Jewish atrocity propaganda: buy only at German shops!*—but there was almost nothing left in her memory to account for her possessing it.

It's just an ordinary little snap, two inches by three. Someone must have given or posted it to her. I found it impossible to imagine such an act taking place with any sentiment implicit other than: this is the situation now, and it can only deteriorate. But what did I know?

'Jolly strange,' she said.

'You don't remember anything? You kept it in a drawer in the spare-room chest of drawers, in an envelope.'

Some people get nasty as they age, but Stella Ramble grows ever softer. Nowadays, for example, her anti-Semitism has completely vanished.

She used to say, as though it were all fact, 'I lived in Brighton during the war. Choked with Jews. They were so yellow they didn't dare face the bombs in London.'

I pressed her on the photograph. It troubled me more than I can explain. I had worked out that the man was a Brown Shirt, and the boy most probably a member of the *Jungvolk* or the *Hitlerjugend*; but this meant nothing to her.

Eventually, in the vaguest way, she mentioned 'Fuesenberg' concentration camp. But there never has been a camp of that name. I went picking after this additional loose thread when I should have been at work. I got nowhere.

Today, as yesterday, as back when I was wondering about the hat-shop photograph, I can't face my work. I'm sitting here but I can't make myself do it. I have pigeons to watch, thoughts to avoid, places not to be.

Is there anyone who would relish writing articles for glossy, in-house magazines, distributed by a central publishing company, probably located in a prefab—I'm guessing, I've never been there—to chains of bizarrely expensive health clubs, hotels, spas, retirement colonies, golf 'awaybreak' centres and so on? I find my job, I mean the idea that I do it—I find it hard to believe.

What is the reason for the word 'hack' being used to describe someone who writes solely for money? Horses again: it dates from the era of the hackney cab. 'Hack' referred originally to the starved and suffering hackney horse, available for hire. The problem for one's soul in hack writing is not the job of the writing itself, but the pose that trash of this kind requires the writer to strike.

Posit, as a mandatory first sentence: *Thinking of getting away in the spring? What goes next?*

Life looking second rate the other side of Xmas? Think twice! Most tour companies promise to make extreme activities safe even for older adventurers but at Dead Right Holidays we've turned this philosophy on its head. Our first four years we successfully killed 216 of our valued customers. And did they complain? As of yet: no. Not a single one complained! (The relaxed atmosphere in our customer complaints division is simply scandalous!) Our most successful single incident took place during a serene coach tour experience with 45 simultaneous drownings effected when a fully-filled 42 seater Dead Right bus plus driver and two guides in Classic Cotswold Country (home of classic Cotswold homes) skidded down a classic Wold hillside setting into freezing lake with No Way Out for dedicated holiday helpers, Gordon Blister, Beverley Planing, Valeria O'Woil, nor 42 elderly Cotswold voyeurs. Prime subaqua viewing greeted these feisty trippers as they brothe their last. Police divers later discovered both executive window hammers 'in place' suggesting death was met with inscrutable pension-age composure. (We're the best: so our customers!) Who wouldn't want to die on a relaxing holiday having the time of your life? For many the answer to this seemingly mindbending conundrum is, Yes! Yes! I want to die happy. Yes! I want to die at my own convenience when convenient to me. Thus was the Dead Right Holidays philosophy begat! So we all die in the end? Look, you don't have to be deaf in one ear with autistic tendencies and a dysfunctional pelvis to start planning now. Turn the page dare you! and check out our value package multideal spring prices for—

How can it possibly be a true fact about me that I ought, as I sit here, to be raving on about Japanese illuminated ice sculptures?

Every February, at the Yuki Matsuri festival, on the island of Hokkaido, in the city of Sapporo, sculptors using Samurai chisels carve tons of blocks of ice. Clear ice is at a premium, but impure ice is also used, as miniature air bubbles and flaws can distort light to startling effect.

Yes! I am a hack! My mind is full of miniature air bubbles and flaws! *Check out our information on value package multideal spring awaybreak prices.*

I know it's déclassé to talk about money, even photocopied money in small denominations, but it happens to be the case that I earn, per month, as a hack, depending on how many words I'm asked to produce, a sum that would cover basic food, a book or two, and a shared-tenancy, one-room rent.

I'm paid by the word. I get a kind of puerile, pie-in-the-eye buzz the more monosyllables I use, because I receive the same number of pennies for writing 'a', as for, whatever, 'misapprehensiveness'. Of course, monosyllables are the tops anyway, so it's win–win; though being expected to write garbage paragraphs in which you pretend to urge people to take an interest in something you only pretend to know about, knowing the chances are nil they will ever really pursue it, makes any quantity of pay an outrage set against the damage done, in the execution of your duty, to your nerves.

Don't get me wrong, as strangers say in pubs, it isn't that I wholly deplore my line of work. For one thing, it has led me, by a hop, skip and a jump, to the curious world of my main man, Edward Lloyd.

Johnson Pike had a very short boyfriend for a spell, called Zed, who was doing a PhD on some aspect of literacy in Victorian England.

'I have to introduce you,' said Johnson.

By the time this meeting came off, the two of them were barely on speaking terms.

It was Zed who told me in passing about Edward Lloyd, king of perfect liars in 1840s England.

I had said—we were in The Hole in the Wall—that my job was affecting my morale more than I could stand, and mentioned that I had looked up and found out that the word 'lie', as we use it in English to mean a falsehood, was over a thousand years old, while the word 'falsehood' went back— Johnson sighed heavily—to around 1300; that 'falsity' then took another three hundred years, while 'fabrication', in this sense, had been with us only a couple of centuries.

'If you go by increasing syllable counts,' I said, 'we can predict that some time around 2100 there'll be a new word for it with five of them.'

I said I thought my job, writing travel articles about places where I've never been, gave advance force to this five-syllable word.

'Contrafactual misrepresentation?' said Zed.

This made me happy. I smiled at him and replied, 'Okay, what's *factual* misrepresentation?'

'Listen,' said Johnson on the phone afterwards, 'do you have to be quite so educational?'

'Are you really dumping him?' I asked. 'I thought he was nice.'

'Don't!' said Johnson. 'Mission totally accomplished. "Nice" is just so—'

After school, I got myself a degree in English, a discipline that interested me less and less the more I understood what was required.

Since my chat with Zed though, I've had a quiet dream of studying Edward Lloyd, somewhere, to whatever end. I would like to have the time to get the measure of Lloyd's lies. Well, I would have the time now, and I could manage it, if I only lived close enough to the right sort of library. The thing is, Con abandoned a PhD on Ravel in order to take up work as an orchestrator. There's more to it than that, of course; but anyway, it irritates him, not that he'd admit it, to think that I might end up better qualified than he is, so he says, 'You can't piss around studying something that's not going to get you a job. You think I do what I do for fun?'

I never have an answer for this, as a result of which, Edward Lloyd has so far been no more than my uncle in the round-house, my bit on the side.

But I have made a start on him.

*

In the 1840s, a government-imposed stamp duty kept the minimum price of an English newspaper at four pence, a sum way beyond any ordinary labourer. In recompense for this tax, supposedly, newspapers could be sent through the post for nothing: the postal system also belonged to the government. By this means, information would wend slowly from the cities into the countryside. It was illegal to perforate or otherwise mark a newspaper so as to send the recipient a coded message, effectively a free letter. It was also illegal to publish any sort of newspaper without paying stamp duty on it. But Edward Lloyd's fabulously successful idea was to print one-penny newspapers that avoided this punishment by virtue of the fact that not a single story in them was true.

Proof of the importance of defining 'news' here can be deduced from his having only narrowly avoided prosecution, on the 8th of January, 1843, when one of his writers accidentally included the genuine story of a lion on the loose in London that had escaped from somebody's zoo.

Within a few years, Lloyd was one of the richest newspapermen in the land. Demand for his product was so high that he had to plant his own forests to generate enough paper.

So, here's the question. If one were compelled by law to fill a penny newspaper with anything but news, avoiding in particular all metropolitan topicality; if one wished to make a fortune out of fantastic, faked stories, bent information and suitable lies, what would be the plan for charming impoverished Londoners of the 1840s into giving up their beer money?—beer, not water, being the cheapest liquid it was safe, at the time, to drink.

It is important to note that you decidedly didn't want to print anything quite so plausible that it provoked the investigative

arm of the law. There was also at this time the offence of 'circu-
lating false news', designed, amongst other things, to prevent
the weary hawker from trying to shift a heap of the day's unsold
papers by yelling out, say, that the Duke of Wellington had just
been struck down dead. You definitely didn't want to be fingered
as an exploitative pseudo-alarmist. That was also a crime.

Lloyd himself came up with several answers to the
constraints imposed by the law. Principally he told tales dressed
up to look like news of long ago. On the 12th of July, 1840,
for example, he had the headline: A COOK BOILED TO DEATH IN
SMITHFIELD. Self-evidently, this is brilliant. And the first four
words of the article? 'In the year 1530—'

Or what about this for front-page news of a shocking
murder? 'A more detestable instance of deliberate ferocity than
the following has rarely disgraced humanity:—On the 25th
April, 1759—' So what if the story was eighty-one years out
of date and had never happened anyway?

Lloyd could get away with news of up-to-date assaults only
if they had taken place in foreign lands, such as the terror
wrought by a bride-eating Philippine alligator. And if he
couldn't resist the English? It seems he was permitted to dish
up stories of the English so long as they were at sea.

One might argue that the English being at sea could hardly
have been thought to constitute news, let alone fake news. I
agree, as, myself, a grade-one example of an English person at
sea. This is not news by any stretch of anybody's imagination.

Nevertheless, Lloyd was wonderful on the subject:

A most unhappy affair has occurred on board the Fitzwilliam
East-Indiaman, just arrived. Mr. R. Dawson and his niece were

passengers in the ship from Bengal, having part of the captain's cabin, or roundhouse, assigned to themselves for accommodation, and lived at the captain's table. The gentleman was a widower, and appeared to be about forty-five years of age, and his niece about thirty: the former had been in the profession of the law, and was reputed to have some fortune, as had the lady, and both were from Yorkshire. On Wednesday morning, the 28th ult., it was currently reported in the ship, that Mr. D. (a cuddy passenger) had, by looking through the key-hole of the door of their apartment, on Tuesday afternoon, discovered them in an improper situation: that he had called another person to be witness to the same; that they alarmed the parties by knocking at the door, and then retired. The affair being universally made known, a reserve took place between the gentleman and the parties, and an explanation was so far gone into as to convince the latter that their guilt was public. They accordingly soon retired from the table, and remained that day and Thursday in their apartment. On Friday morning, the 30th, upon a servant knocking at the door, and not being able to obtain admittance or attention, a suspicion arose, and the gunner was desired to go over the ship's quarter, and look into their apartment, on which he discovered that they had destroyed themselves. The gentleman was found sitting in the quarter gallery, with a fusee and a pistol, with the latter of which he had shot himself through the head; the lady was lying in the balcony with a discharged pistol near her, with which she had shattered her head in a shocking manner. They had been dead some time, and it was about seven in the morning when this part of the melancholy business was publicly known in the ship. Their bodies were committed to the deep at mid day.

Some letters were found written by the lady, addressed to several friends and relations: one to the captain, thanking him for his kindness; one to the person whose fatal curiosity had occasioned the discovery, upbraiding him with his cruel officiousness; and one to a gentleman in the same ship, who had paid his addresses to her, assuring him that she esteemed him highly; but declaring, that it never was her intention to impose on him a woman whose conduct had rendered her unworthy of him.

So, this story is made up; and yet, how distressing it is, still, to read of *cruel officiousness*, of *reserves* taking place, of *shockingly shattered heads*.

What I don't understand is why the phrase 'at sea' implies incapacity and limitation. Surely, for the English, being at sea ought to mean being exhilaratingly in conversation with the waves and the stars, the stars and the waves, the fish, the wind, the salt, the spray. Didn't we *rule* the waves once upon a time? No? Don't tell me we crept out onto our great oak ships and stood around, embarrassed, as little gusty breezes sank the Spanish Armada.

Oh well, I have to observe that if you are drawn to old newspapers, especially ones that were required to be pure invention, then the daily papers of your own age come to seem utterly ridiculous, *let alone* the narrative of your own life.

There's a reason Lloyd became rich enough to plant his own forests:

At an Indian wedding in the Philippine Islands, the bride retired from the company to go down to the river and wash her feet, as is customary. As she was thus employed, an alligator of the largest kind seized her. Her shrieks brought the people to the place, who saw her between the monster's teeth, and just drawn under the water. The bridegroom instantly plunged in, and with his dagger in his hand, pursued the monster. After a desperate conflict, he made him deliver up his prey, and swam to the shore with the body of his dead wife in his arms.

!*Bam*!

I suppose it's a reasonable question why I'm sitting here going on about alligators, instead of, I don't know, phoning my mother; but if I were to tell her that my marriage has ground to a halt—because I'm useless &c., a vampire, deaf, borderline anti-social, a hater of music, unsupportive, intermittently speechless &c.—if I were to tell her that Con has given up and disappeared, she would listen to every word and then say, 'Who is she?'.

That's what my mother would say, and protest on my part would be futile. 'Who is she?' Protest would be futile. This is my mother's area. In this department, as in many others, I feel sure she regards me as a *fucking amateur*.

My parents had a bad marriage so it always stood to reason that I was hardly likely to have a good one.

My mother has a habit of saying, 'I must be completely mad', as in, 'I must be completely mad, I forgot to change the sheets,' or, 'I must be completely mad, I didn't set the alarm clock.' By normal standards, she has never come anywhere close to madness, unless you take the arch position on the English bourgeoisie that its members so thoroughly miss the point of life, only madness can explain it.

I remember very clearly the day, I was about twelve, when

she mumbled to herself, 'I must be completely mad, I'm sleeping with a married man.'

Since then she has been the mistress of a number of married men. This is her area, or at least, it became her area after my father left, or, I think that's the way the thing worked.

Johnson claims to worship my mother and accuses me of being too straight to appreciate her. If that's what the impediment is, I am. Another of her phrases is, 'as easy as falling out of bed', but here again I suspect her. How many people would have no qualms about falling out of bed? Beds wouldn't be designed as they are if people endlessly fell out of them.

~

It's hours, now, since Mrs Shaw came and got me. She beat at the door, and in her growliest voice said, 'We're going out, remember?'

I hadn't remembered. I had no excuses at the ready. It was so warm I didn't even need to put on a cardigan.

Within minutes we were walking down the street together. Well, I lolloped. She had changed into a different pair of heels, delicate green.

She said, 'How d'you get the gimpy legs then?'

I replied, 'It's the after-effects of septic arthritis coupled with a dysfunctional pelvis.'

'Bloody hell,' said Mrs Shaw.

I had to do a double take to work out that she then, with impressive accuracy, spat the gum she'd been chewing into the municipal litter bin outside Brown's Shoppe. It crossed my mind that the ten-pound-note man had perhaps used the same bin for the A4 he must have torn away to make his photocopied money—KEEP BRITAIN TIDY. I checked the lime trees: no leaf fall worth mentioning. Well, absolutely no leaf fall whatsoever.

We gimped along to find a pair of policemen standing in the doorway to the pub.

'Screw it,' muttered Mrs Shaw.

When you step into The Admiral, the world goes dark, air quality plummets and your feet sink into a deep blue, slightly adhesive carpet with anchors on.

I half saw a man at the bar glance at us. I didn't make out whether he had looked at me, because I'm a cripple, or at Mrs Shaw, because she's pretty, or at both of us together, because we didn't match. Probably he was just looking at Mrs Shaw.

She asked me whether I'd like a pint or what, and I said I'd get it.

'No no, you're all right,' she said, and gestured with her thumb at a chair—almost, I'm not sure, solicitously.

She came back with two pints and two chasers, of all things, rum. As she sat down, I asked her why she didn't like policemen.

'Screw it,' she said again.

She got out a cigarette and held it unlit between her fingers.

I felt agitated but said nothing. At my worst, this feeling sometimes causes me to become garrulous; not now, though.

Mrs Shaw took a long drink of beer and said, 'Used to like them when I was a kid. I come from a good family. Before she had us lot, right, my mum was a counter clerk at Handley's. She says it was an easy lay, but I know she had to slog at it. And my dad used to be an engineer, but he was a drunk, a champagne alcoholic, la-di-da-di-da, expensive, so we never had no money, right, and he was always being arrested but he was a *happy drunk.*'

She broke off to light the cigarette and then started up again.

'I know what you're thinking but anyway he was, right, and the police used to bring him home, and we liked them because they got him home so he didn't always end up in the gutter if you know what I mean. They all knew him. So my sister, when she was fourteen, right, she got raped, right, by this bloke off the estates, right, and she got pregnant, and my mum wouldn't let it go to court, she's like, "I'm not having people looking at her." So the police round our way, they was friends with my dad so they picks up the bloke what done it and they takes him on *a trip around the world*, you know? They puts him in the back of one of their vans, right, and they drives him all over Bedford, going on every street in Bedford, and they beats the total fucking shit out of him.'

In my mind for some reason I translated this into the phrase, 'They thrashed him to within an inch of his life.'

It became increasingly hard for me to make out Mrs Shaw's speech, not only because she had the cigarette wagging between her lips, but because whenever she removed it she let smoke spill out of her mouth like tide waters flooding a gully.

She drank her way far down her glass, temporarily lost in thought.

I said to myself: hey *gimpy* legs, two days ago you were as happily married as anyone, and now you're sitting in The Admiral with a stranger from Bedford talking about rapists.

There was a crash of coins plus a happy-music jingle as someone in the corner struck lucky on the slot machine.

'He died falling downstairs.'

Well, I thought that was what she said. 'Who?' I asked, and prepared to unravel her reply.

Her lipstick was so worn away that it provided only an outline to her mouth. I couldn't quite imagine why she hadn't filled in the shape before setting out from home.

'My dad,' she said.

'That's really odd,' I said. 'My father died falling downstairs as well.'

'He was drunk,' said Mrs Shaw.

'Nobody knows for definite whether my father killed himself on purpose or not,' I said, but she wasn't interested, and I didn't want to talk about it if she wasn't interested.

All the same, this was the first time I'd met someone else whose father died falling down the stairs. With my father, the story is that he said, 'I'll see myself out,' walked the few steps to the top of the staircase in question, and then fell, at once, to his death.

'Why don't you like the police now?' I asked.

'Leave it out.' Mrs Shaw leant forwards so that her breasts sat on the table top. 'That with my dad, that was way back. Police ain't the same no more. My life now—Micky can't put a foot out the door in Bedford without hassle, know what I mean? My mum give us the money to get out for a breather so we come here and now what? Your fucking husband, that's what. If you'd've kept him happy—' Her voice rose to a note of real anger.

The landlord, George, switched on the television, which was up behind me, perched on a thin shelf just below the ceiling. From here on out, my conversation with Mrs Shaw was accompanied by intermittent cheering.

'—swiped the green stuff and gone off to Majorca by myself.'

'Why do you say I didn't keep him happy?' I asked.

'Don't blame me,' she replied casually. 'I didn't say nothing, he said it.'

'He what—what? When?' I wanted not to respond to her provocations but couldn't help myself. And I kept asking the wrong questions.

'You just chucked him out, right?' Mrs Shaw spoke with a shade of contempt that made me wonder whether she wasn't enjoying herself.

'What?'

She laughed derisively—a low, dirty, derisive sort of laugh. 'Your git of a husband was up at the bar, little while back, and you was sat over there,' she tilted her head towards our usual table, 'and he has his wallet hanging out his back pocket like a bloody collawold,'—*collawold*?—'so Micky's like, he can't resist himself from fingering it, but, stupid git catches him. That's when bloody everything starts going tit arsewards.'

'I was here?'

'You don't notice nothing, right?' said Mrs Shaw. 'That's one reason your husband's gone AWOL on you, right?'

With foolish earnestness, I said, 'He—I didn't throw him out.'

'Well, what the fuck does it matter, you know?' said Mrs Shaw. 'In the end, you know? "Her and me," he goes, "we're not off of the same planet, right? She don't notice nothing." He's going, like, what he said, right, he's sick of all—'

I had stopped watching her speak and there was an eruption on the TV. I strugglingly heard, '—sick of all your inner qualities.'

The television cheering went on and on. I tried to loop

back through Mrs Shaw's words to make them come good.

The picture of Con talking about me like this to outsiders—it hadn't crossed my mind that, while I didn't plan to tell anybody anything, Con might have told every man, bird and cat about our maladjusted life together; and not only that, but that he might have set to lying about it.

For the first time since he'd gone, for a split second, I thought I might cry.

When I don't notice what's happening around me, Con sometimes says, 'Hey Ramble, you're falling asleep at the wheel.'

He's sick of all your *inequalities*, I thought. Could this have been it? If so, what exactly—if—

I was, I realised—and realised I had been for some time—shunting my empty rum glass back and forth in the wet of spilled beer on the table top.

I stood up straight away and said, 'I'm going.' I ought to have offered to buy Mrs Shaw a drink, she'd bought me two, but I didn't do it. I looked at her hands. She had no rings on, not a wedding band, nothing. I was still wearing mine.

She said, 'Don't mind me. I'm a bit rough,' stood up also and followed me out.

It was cold, for a moment, stepping out of the pub.

As we walked the short distance home, Mrs Shaw said, 'We only got the place downstairs of you because your husband fixed it.'

Why would the collapse of my marriage be anything to do with the people downstairs? I had no answer to this, and was distracted by birdsong, because, with all England at its disposal, a blackbird had chosen to sit in the lime tree outside our building and was singing its liquid heart out in the sodium darkness.

To myself or to Mrs Shaw, I said, 'I don't want to know anything.'

She had the grace not to reply.

The hallway felt sepulchral.

'Can you hear us fighting?' Mrs Shaw waved dismissively at the door to her flat.

'Oh.' I pretended to ponder the question. 'You do some-times shout.'

Apart from stairs being one of my worst things, I was tipsy enough after the drinks, on no proper sleep or food, to find it imperative to grip the banisters hand over hand as I made my way up.

In time, I reached the small landing at the top. I didn't know why Mrs Shaw was still following me. She clicked patiently in my wake.

'Right—' She tried to speak but started laughing instead, a laugh so dirty and infectious that I missed getting the key into the flat door lock and there I was leaning against the wall half out of control with laughter myself, the tears welling up again. Jesus, I thought, I'm smashed, depressed, knackered and worn to pieces, and I don't want to cry and I think I'm about to. Yet it was so pleasant to laugh that I couldn't stop, even being afraid I might cry. I had no idea what the joke was, not the shred of an idea. This seemed funny in itself.

Through her own laughter, Mrs Shaw finally stuttered out, '—know how, right, every bloke in—the world, right, wants to come up behind his bird—' her hilarity engulfed her and she stalled again before willing herself on, '—wants to come up behind his bird and fuck her while she's doing the washing up?'

I took a deep breath and accidentally squeaked, 'Yes.'

'So, right, Friday, he gets it on and he's hands everywhere, right, and I'm washing up and I gets fed up, right, and I, I has this saucepan,' again she broke down ungovernably before gasping, 'right, what I'm washing up—right,' the phrase 'washing up' made my knees bend, '—so I just turns around and I bloody whacks him over the head with it and—' the tears were sliding down Mrs Shaw's cheeks now as well as mine—she was barely able to speak, '—and, bloody hell, I've only gone and knocked him out!'

We both laughed so much, so helplessly, that we too wound up slumped down on the floor.

Christ and Christ again, I've just noticed that it's past three in the morning. The temperature has dipped to its lowest for days. I'm sitting here wrapped in our yellow blanket—we have two blankets—with my arms all chilly where they're poking out.

My head hurts.

I just saw an improbable vision. The window is open. I can't bring myself to stand up, lean over and close it, so nothing but air was between me and what struck my eye as a medium-weight bird of prey gliding lethally up the street.

If it was some optical trick, I don't know what else could have looked so like a buzzard. Does a plastic bag have sinews and a beak? Round here, this thing should have been a deranged pigeon, but it certainly wasn't.

I do know why a buzzard would be what my eye took it for. The summer I was seventeen, when I was still a schoolgirl, and my legs still worked, my mother sent me to stay with a cast-off lover of hers at his farm chateau in the south of France. She thought I might want to pitch in on the land, or read a stack of books, I don't know.

'If nothing else, it'll do you no end of good to get out of England,' she said.

'Why?' I asked.

I felt, in this phase of my life, that the world the grown-ups lived in was so far removed from my own that I would never be able to cross the line that separated me from them; and there was still some sort of childish hope in me that I was therefore safe.

The *patron* of the chateau and his busy wife, I think my mother described her as 'hectic', had a man from Portsmouth working for them. He lived in one of the partly derelict buildings that leant against the castle wall. He had done time in the army so he knew how to drive heavy vehicles, as well as fix them.

In that part of the world, you booked to use specialist tractors and other such equipment seasonally. If you found you needed to overrun your allotted hire period: bad luck. On the given day, all the machinery would be lumberingly driven off to the next place in line. Farmers panicked and talked incessantly about their odds of beating the tight timetables threatened by the weather. It was an area of the south that had the most spectacular storms, with pink lightning.

The way they organised themselves down there, it was accepted that there were times in the year when farm work might have to continue well after sunset. When I was staying, a vast sloping field had to be put to the disc across an entire night.

I knew the man from Portsmouth was an ex-convict. He had

told me about it over a sandwich. After the army, he'd been done for attempted murder. He'd got into a dispute defending somebody else's wife in some way, and when one of the men on the opposite side of the question had chased him and smashed through the passenger window of his car with a pool cue, he'd grabbed hold of this man with his left hand and had driven, steering with his right, against a long line of parked cars.

'What was I supposed to do?' he said to me. 'Cunt was trying to take my head off.'

When he requested that I sit in the back of the tractor cab all night to keep him awake, the only thing I could think was that I was about to spend the night with a man who was almost a murderer.

As we went along, he told me at great length about the different patterns for ploughing a straight-edged field, the problem being the curves you are forced to make when you turn, set against the need to plough every possible inch, while minimising the fuel waste involved in going twice over the same patch of ground.

This puzzle was pretty well just noise to me, but I was unable to go to sleep myself as the little ledge I was sitting on wasn't designed for this purpose, and the tractor rocked so much over the parched earth that I had continually to press my arms against the insides of the windows to prevent myself toppling about. Before long, I was in pain.

To compensate for this bodily distress, I was able to watch lozenge-shaped owls swooping in and out of the two powerful beams of the tractor headlamps as we moved through the deep, dense darkness: the churning steel discs inflicted Armageddon on each mouse and lizard that lived in the dust on the uppermost edge of this world, so we were attended remorselessly by hunting birds.

After hours and hours, a dim light began to stain the eastern firmament, and the owls retired to be replaced by other birds of prey that I didn't precisely recognise, but thought of as buzzards. Come dawn, I could see that a great cloud of them followed in our wake, and reaped using fistfuls of talons.

In the cool of the evening, you would find these buzzards still adrift on the thermals thrown skywards by the burning-hot tarmac roads. I'm going on as though I know what I'm talking about. This is the full extent of my knowledge on the subject.

Anyway, how did I avoid sleeping with the man from Portsmouth? At, I don't know what, past five sometime, with the sun above the horizon and the field nearly done, I said, 'I must be completely mad, I forgot to turn off my alarm clock.'

We were out of the climate-controlled cab breathing the fresh, sharp, disturbed smell of the field's own air, pausing, as we had done at roughly three-hour intervals, to stretch our legs. Without explaining further, I turned and staggered away across the broken-up sod the long distance to the verge, and over it, side-stepping a snake-sized branch that lay on one of the paths—it had just the look of a snake waiting for the sun to warm it into action. Then I ran, as my own system began to reconfigure itself into a functioning unit, I ran away from my new friend towards the chateau up the hill.

'Thank you,' said the *patron* that afternoon. 'Thank you. Honestly speaking, I don't know that we'd have got the field done without your help.'

For a few days, there were tiny courteous gestures shown me by my hosts that allowed for the possibility that I was having a fling with their convict. Then they decided that this wasn't it at all, and the little gestures ceased.

The best thing about the man from Portsmouth was his silver Ford Cortina, once upon a time the car with the highest accident rate in England.

I find it peculiar, as I sit here, that for the second night in a row Mrs Shaw is downstairs on the sofa. The pink blanket was still where she'd left it. Perhaps I should unwrap one of Bobbo Stothard's throat-constricting soaps and put it out in the bathroom for tomorrow morning.

Mrs Shaw hit Mr Shaw with the saucepan on Friday evening, then spent the whole of that night sitting on a little table in the main room in her flat, she told me, afraid that if she fell asleep he'd 'sort her out'.

Last night—feeling pissed off, she implied, and I can vouch for it—she took the precaution of coming upstairs and asking to sleep here. *Amateur what?* I've forgotten to ask again.

This evening, after we'd finished our big joke on the landing, she informed me that it had been because she'd had no sleep on Friday, 'That's why I fall asleep so sudden when you had me in last night.'

'But you did see me get the beer from the kitchen,' I said. 'What?'

'How did you know I'd like a beer?' I asked.

'What?' she said. 'You was in the pub. I told you.'

Mrs Shaw explained to me, as you do to someone off another planet, that usually when she hit her husband she went to stay with her mother for a couple of nights until the thing blew over.

'Why don't you go back to Bedford now?'

'Not that I want to, but I ain't got the money,' she said. 'Can I nick the sofa again tonight? I won't do it tomorrow.'

'Is he downstairs?' I asked

'Don't know,' she said. 'They've buggered off together, yours and mine. Don't know where they are. But I don't know when they're coming back neither.'

'Why could he not have sorted you out if you were awake?' I asked, as though this were any old question.

I was thinking: when *they're* coming back?

Mrs Shaw grinned. She didn't speak for a while. I glanced at her and for the first time took in that one of her lower teeth is chipped. 'Tell you what,' she said at last, 'he wouldn't dare.'

My French stay was unsettling, the buzzards and the lightning storms &c., and not really understanding what was expected of me; but it was because of this visit that I got my job.

Con used to have a friend whom I thought of as the Kronenbourg Guy—now I come to say this, I don't know what's happened to him. Whenever they met for a drink, which wasn't that often, they would pretend to be strangers. One of them would elbow or bash into the other, hard enough to raise eyebrows along the bar, and they would go through the following exchange.

'Hey, what's your problem?'

'What's yours?'

'I'll have a Kronenbourg, thanks.'

The Kronenbourg Guy showed up one evening with a girl who had been solicited by my present employers, I don't remember what the connection was, to do a kind of gingham-curtain travel piece on French chateau living. That very afternoon she'd been dismayed to discover, having accepted the job, that it wouldn't involve actually going anywhere.

'Who do they think they are?' she said, sounding sincerely exasperated.

The way it unfolded, she ended up asking me whether I, as a notional specialist, would like to toss the piece off instead.

At the time I thought it would be amusing to pretend to know what I was talking about; plus, not having to go somewhere suited me fine.

Naturally, none of the information I had at my disposal—tractors, Portsmouth Jail, Ford Cortinas and so on—was of the slightest use to me in writing the article required, but as early as job number two, my employers dropped the pretence that they had ever thought I knew what I was talking about anyway. And it doesn't matter. It doesn't matter a bit. When they like what you come up with, when they like your writing, they say, 'Nice pictures.' What these people crave is *nice pictures*.

It's rising four. I must go to sleep. I'm in pain from sitting up for so long and I'm chilly. For all the recent heat, it isn't pleasant to be this cold. I feel tired the way I felt tired when my father fell down the stairs.

I haven't mentioned this, but all day long I've had these ugly noises in my head.

If I ever knew what I was doing, I definitely don't know now, although, the reason I'm just sitting here, still, is that I don't want to go to bed. I don't want to go to bed. Great, fine, wonderful: that's what I'm doing sitting here. But I don't know what I'm doing, even so.

3

Monday

I woke up this morning overwhelmed again, wishing that I, too, had been killed on my wedding day by an alligator of the largest kind.

Given my circumstances, this would more or less have had to take place at a zoo. The way I picture it, my blood is gushing fatally from multiple puncture wounds into a government-approved alligator pond filled with very cheerful alligators, and there's no groom plunging in with a dagger. I'd like to think that in my final, agonised moments, against a backdrop of spectator shrieks &c., I'd be cherishing the hope that a century on, some vampire like me, lodged in Colindale Newspaper Library to research, say, turn-of-the-century sewerage—that this person, having inattentively passed over my death notice in what has become an antique copy of a local news sheet, would pause, and reread with a comic expression, to check that he'd got it right.

My second thought was that I would prefer the alligators to have killed Con. After his spiel on Saturday, I haven't inclined to think much about anything in him I ever, quietly, liked.

Why did I marry him? I don't really know. He persuaded me it was the brave thing to do.

I was jolted into consciousness by his alarm clock. Usually I wake several minutes before it goes off, and to avoid the racket, as swiftly as possible hobble my way down to the kitchen. I say hobble. On an ordinary day, my walking is at its absolute worst when I've just got out of bed. I have asked Con more than once if it would be possible to alter our system of getting up, but somehow nothing's ever changed; and now, even less explicably, I can't bring myself to disable his clock, just as I haven't yet taken off my wedding ring, washed up our last lunch together or thrown away the orange peel.

The alarm clock woke me to chaotic thoughts and a sense of foreboding. I slid out of bed, blundered over here to the table and for some time simply sat and looked at the pigeons.

I sat and considered pigeons, alligators, orange peel, alarm clocks—regarding the last of which: when I mentioned that I ran away from the man from Portsmouth saying, 'I must be completely mad, I forgot to turn off my alarm clock,' this was untrue. I don't mean untrue that I said such a thing, but untrue that I'd forgotten to turn it off. I didn't possess an alarm clock.

My mind crawled nervously about. From clock alarms, it slipped sideways to how there's a standard sign that gets pasted on glass fire doors these days that says, WARNING! NO EXIT. THESE DOORS ARE ALARMED. *Wretched* doors, I said to myself, peering over at an elderly gent across the road, who plumped himself down in the more stable of the two white moulded-plastic chairs that live on the pavement outside the minicab office.

A girl at my school had a great-aunt who was blind, who died as a result of walking through a plate-glass door. That door was *shattered*. The first time I heard about it, my imagination did a sort of narrative double take. Of course it sounded terrific, but isn't it the case that death-by-plate-glass-door is truly piquant only if the person who cops it this way fails to notice the danger despite being able to *see*?

I'm recording this nonsense when what I need to do is make myself a coffee.

~

I went downstairs and was surprised to discover Mrs Shaw still here, awake, still lying on the sofa. I had expected to find only the pink blanket. Had this been a sequence in a movie, with a music cue as I tottered down the stairs, the composer would doubtless have primed the audience for the fact that I was going to walk in on Mrs Shaw and be surprised.

Her posture suggested lack of will.

'Coffee?'

'Wouldn't say no.'

'Milk?'

'Cheers.'

I went through into the kitchen, set the coffee going and got out our milk frother, a manual device with a mesh disc and wooden handle.

I haven't been positively compelled to do the washing up since Con left, two days ago now, because I've been subsisting on biscuits and coffee. I'm drinking so much of the stuff, it leaves a taste in my mouth like ashes. Naturally I've rinsed the coffee maker and my cup several times, but I'm ashamed to say that in all other respects, I've left the kitchen untouched.

Mrs Shaw frowned at the grimy plates on the grimy table, shifted them to the washing-up bowl, threw away the orange peel and sat down. She'd put her ethereal green heels back on.

In no time the smell of cooking coffee overtook the weary smell of our bodies.

'Got a lot of books,' she said, gesturing through the doorway back into the main room.

The three-in-one sofa sits in front of a wall that's floor to ceiling books. Con made the shelves out of cheap planks, with pilfered bricks as dividers.

There are bricks all over the place round here. If there's ever the need for a riot, it won't be many minutes before the windows of the neighbourhood have all gone smash.

'The early Victorian stuff and the literature's mostly mine,' I said, 'but some of them are my husband's. He got part way through a PhD on Ravel—the composer—*Bolero*? He studied him for a couple of years. Those sorts of books are his, the music stuff; and some of the rest.'

'You talking university?' said Mrs Shaw.

'Yes, yes, university.'

'My sister went to university,' she said. I said nothing, but she added, 'Not her. Different sister.'

'Oh, I didn't—realise, I didn't know. What did she read?'

Mrs Shaw rolled my question round her mind for a long time before answering, and when finally she spoke, it was in tones that implied I was completely stupid, which led me to *feel* completely stupid.

'Books,' she said.

I was trembling as I put her cup of coffee in front of her. I'd managed to get the milk froth in a peak above the rim.

'Somebody's keen,' she remarked, but I think she was pleased.

'Sugar?'

I said 'sugar', and was reminded, from nowhere, of an anecdote my grandfather told me years ago: my mother's father. One day he went on a job somewhere new, further from home than made economic sense, but anyway. He was a piano tuner. He had a high notion of piano tuners. He would lay it out from time to time that, back in the days when the better sort of house had a separate entrance for tradesmen, the piano tuner would be expected at the front door. In those days, well-tuned pianos were crucial to the happiness of the more comfortable classes. Piano tuners were thought of as above trade, he explained; in his opinion, rightly so.

The drive was taking a while. He saw signs for a service stop and pulled in. He went into the café, ordered a cup of tea, found himself a table and sat down. As he waited, he saw that the men who came in after him all lingered at the counter for their orders, and carried their cups, plates or glasses to their tables themselves.

Grandfather was debating going back up to collect his order when the manageress came out front. She plonked a cup of tea down on his table. There was milk in it already. 'You want sugar in that?' she asked, and he said, 'Thanks but no thanks.'

Grandfather broke off when he reached this place in the story. 'I knew what she was going to say next, it's an old one, but I let her because she was ugly.'

'You knew?' I said.

He smiled at me and put on a hoity-toity waitress voice. 'You want sugar in your tea? No? *Don't stir it then.*'

I was a child. I thought about this hard. 'Do you mean you wouldn't have let her say that if she'd been beautiful?'

'Ah, well now,' he said, 'that changes the case. Because— well, say she'd been knockout drops? Then I'd have stayed up at the counter.'

'*If* you've got any,' said Mrs Shaw, for the second time, I slowly realised.

I found a bag of sugar behind a bag of rice.

How I had wished, talking to Grandfather, that I might grow up to be knockout drops.

My mother has a high notion not of piano tuners, but of herself. When she drinks a cup of tea or coffee, instead of resting the rim against the inside of her lower lip like the average human being, she sits it against the tip of her tongue. I assume this is to stop her lipstick smudging, and have asked myself whether it is for the same reason that she doesn't ever kiss me warmly.

Another curious fact about my mother is that she has an expressionless face, though she makes up for this by the way she talks. I've spent hours of my life thumbing through the magazines she buys, and I think she must have trained herself not to expostulate, grin or visibly suffer, after reading advice on how to avoid an excess of wrinkles.

That said, she is deeply lined. I think she acquires her lines in her sleep, having bad dreams.

She's developed a new quirk recently. She keeps an ultra-slim mobile phone in her left-side bra cup. Don't ask me why. Johnson's going to be thrilled when I tell him.

I'm sure Stella Ramble had my mother down as a parvenue the minute they met. Doesn't *The Piano Tuner's Daughter* sound like the title of the kind of novel that sells in post offices?

As for the piano tuner's wife, my mother's mother: when I was three, she died of a burst spleen. People used to shake their heads over how fitting this was. She was a temperamental woman who'd been known in the family since World War II, with affection I might add, as the Bangalore Torpedo—a form of pipe bomb, I recently discovered, used to blow up barbed-wire entanglements.

Grandfather didn't go looking for new clients, they came to him. Contented piano owners recommended him on. 'Better that way,' he would note smugly, as though other men of business had a thing or two to learn.

It was an upshot of this system that many of the people for whom he worked, and in whose houses he spent an hour or so per year, were acquainted with one another. Grandfather liked to describe how he would sometimes walk into house X and recognise the wrong Mr So-and-so hastily buttoning up as he skulked towards the front door. Grandfather wasn't one for *cruel officiousness*, but how was the wrong Mr So-and-so to know that? There would be a gruff appeal to him to keep things under his hat, with sometimes a tenner exchanged in a handshake.

*

Mrs Shaw is my guest, I said to myself, I must make conversation. I could see unusually clearly the dust and odd particles of litter adrift on the floor, the filth on the tiles behind the oven, the cracks in the walls, the ugly plastic lampshade hanging from the ceiling.

Before I could say anything, she declared, 'Personally, I have an ignorance towards books. Don't ask me nothing about books. I only read magazines.'

'I write for the magazines,' I said at once. 'That's my job.'

'Kidding me,' said Mrs Shaw. 'What ones?'

I hoped I wouldn't lose cachet by showing her. I have an unfiled heap of them on one of the counters right there in the kitchen, where they sit like beached jetsam above a swill of more mobile rubbish.

Johnson finds this kind of thing tiresome, but it pleases me to know that, technically speaking, 'jetsam' is the matter you throw out of a ship when you're afraid it's about to sink; whereas, if the ship sinks anyway and is destroyed by the tides, 'flotsam' is the debris of the smashed vessel itself.

I have to hope my work is jetsam.

I showed Mrs Shaw my writing name in a couple of contents lists. I never have used my real name in print. It struck me that she might not know what I'm called—we haven't introduced ourselves—but if she did find my writing name strange, she didn't say so.

'Kidding me,' she repeated, and took the magazines and began to flick her way through. In tones of genial sarcasm she selected a passage from one of my pieces and started to read it aloud. '*These stations can be thought of simply as portals through which you pass into almost-stranded cities. But with faded survivals of 1920s decor lost amid Communist con-crete, they provide their own sense of the revolutionary—'*

I resumed breathing only when she gave up. What had I meant by *almost-stranded*? I had no idea.

The benchmark phrase for hack travel writing is, 'resplendent in its diversity'. Rajasthan, Venice, Peru: resplendent in their &c. &c. A hack wouldn't want to write a line about a place that wasn't—the surface of the moon, for example. First, the reader is taken to have a short attention span, !*bam*!, and second, it wouldn't be *nice pictures*. Maybe an asteroid belt, perhaps, I'm not exactly sure, but definitely not the surface of the moon.

'You been to all these places, then?' Mrs Shaw was looking at the nice pictures.

'It doesn't work like that.'

'Shame,' she said. I was about to say more when she added crossly, 'What, you make it up?'

I wanted to ask her about Con, or rather, I wanted to know more without having to ask.

I tried to think of a question but nothing suitable came to me. I said to myself: she'll get up and leave soon, and then you'll regret not having asked her whatever it is.

This didn't help.

Only a few months before my father, Middleton Ramble, fell down the stairs, Con began to talk about him in tones that suggested it was an understood thing he was weak. In particular, Con implied that Middleton had somehow willed arthritis on himself to short-circuit the disappointments of his performing career. But I don't believe my father was disappointed by his performing career. He once said of his arthritis,

'Why not me?' And this was how he seemed to view his professional engagements also. Why *not* me?

There's a chilling English institution, the concert held at a
local theatre during which a soloist you haven't heard of, and
whose name you make no attempt to remember, gives an excellent performance of a concerto backed by a dead-weight amateur
orchestra. This sort of gig, with audiences made up of the very
best philistines, constituted my father's most rewarding form of
employment. It follows that he played, in the main, for himself.

I think Con grew frightened by my father's example. Con
feels tainted by any association with self-sufficient unsuccess.
He sometimes rants on that all the jobs in film music carry
conspiratorial or menacing titles: composer, arranger, orchestrator, player, fixer, mixer. This is when he's feeling bad about
being the orchestrator.

The precise way a music cue is scored can do a great deal
to slew the impact of a scene; but how many film directors
think about the worker who holds this subtle degree of sway
over the end product? Orchestrators are amongst the lowest
of the low to those who make movies.

If the official composer hasn't the time, can't be bothered, or,
in some cases, isn't competent to rough out much more than
the tunes &c., and if an orchestrator is used, where does he sit
in the credits? He may be listed before the negative cutter, but
he'll usually be after best boy grip, dolly grip, second second
assistant director, re-recording mixer, *hair stylist*. He may be above
the negative cutter, but he's usually after practically everyone else.

Who even reads the credits that far? Most movies have a
closing music cue that starts in the last scenes, spills over the
beginning of the end titles, and then changes tack midway

through to a completely different style of piece. This abrupt shift is known in the trade—obviously the term goes way back—as the 'hat-grabber'. And sure enough, the majority of people in a cinema audience, without knowing why, rise up and clear the building, zombie-like, when the hat-grabber comes on. It deliberately spoils the mood. One of the most efficient ways to achieve this effect is to switch to an irrelevant song.

Anyway, in the language of film music itself, the orchestrator's credit falls way past the hat-grabber, and that's all anyone needs to know about how orchestrators are treated.

I watched as Mrs Shaw shuffled my magazines into a neat pile.

'You like writing this stuff?' she asked.

'Not really. It's a job, that's all.'

'What do you like doing?'

'I don't know. What do you like doing?'

'Don't know,' she said. 'I like watching people have babies on TV.'

I had the railway-departures-board sensation in my mind, but this time the thousand little flaps turned over blank.

'Satellite,' she said.

I exhaled.

'They have this American channel,' her voice grew animated, 'where you watch people going up to having their babies and then you see it in the birthing suite. I love that, right, when it's come out, holding it. Thing is is, like, if you've had a baby, no one can take it away from you.'

I'm extremely glad I was looking at the floor when I replied, 'Well, I believe, you know, in some cases they do.'

Just for a moment, Mrs Shaw was scarily caustic. 'I'm not

thick,' she said. 'No one can take it away from you that you *had* it, that's what I'm saying. You know what? They've found out half the kids in London don't belong to their real dads.' She let loose with her dirty laugh.

'What is that—' I couldn't think and then remembered, 'no, yes, *never comment on a likeness*. But—but by "real", do you mean the man who actually fathered the child, or the man who thought he did?'

Mrs Shaw assessed my question, then said, 'I don't hold with none of this genetic piss artist whatever. Reckon the bloke what brings you up is your real dad, if he's the one what's done all the work, all said and done.'

'I don't think you can dismiss the whole of genetics as rubbish,' I replied.

Before I could cap this pointless remark with further pointless remarks, the phone went.

I stepped round into the other room—the pink blanket was once again neatly folded. On the nature–nurture front, I wondered to myself whether, if the Bangalore Torpedo hadn't died when I was three, she might have been able to instil in me some of her combativeness. I'm not conscious that I've inherited any. I hesitated to pick up the phone, doubly wary for knowing Mrs Shaw would hear.

'Hello, darling. Are you there? It's your mother.'

'You aren't my mother, you're my grandmother,' I said, 'but that's okay. You're Middleton's mother and I'm Middleton's daughter, so I'm your granddaughter—you don't have a daughter—you're my grandmother.'

I was being much too confusing. I could hear a nurse in the background saying, 'Alrighty then, Mrs Ramble?'

'Silly me.' Stella Ramble had a smile in her voice. 'Now, darling, when am I going to see you? I can't find my bag.'

'I'll come and see you tomorrow and find it.'

'Splendid!' she said, and then thought, and then asked me, 'What?'

'Your bag.'

'Can't you find it now?'

'No, I'm not with you, I'm on the other end of the tele-phone.' I was on the other end of the telephone looking down at the lime trees, wishing for a breath of the air that fluttered through their foliage. It might have cooled in the night, but already the day was over-warm again.

'And how's the little girl?'

'*I'm* the little girl,' I said—we sometimes talk like this for extended periods—'that's me, except I've grown up. Guess what? I'm a grown-up now.'

'Go on,' she said.

'It's true, really. It's true. So look, how about we say I'm coming tomorrow? Is that good?'

'Perfect. I shall look forward to it.'

'Bye then.'

'Bye bye, darling. Just remind me so I can write it down.'

'Tomorrow. Tomorrow is Tuesday. Today is Monday. I'll come on Tuesday.'

I didn't bother to mention to her that she's no longer able to write.

To my consternation, Mrs Shaw was washing up, the plates from Saturday and everything. I hadn't heard the taps running.

'That was my grandmother,' I said.

'She off her rocker then?'

I searched for a good answer. 'Well—she's in the bracket of spending hours sorting individual cornflakes into heaps of males and females.'

This wasn't strictly true, but I hoped it would sound amusing, and was gratified that Mrs Shaw, caught by surprise, choked on her own laughter.

Had Stella Ramble ever *not* been off her rocker? I asked myself. When I cleared out her house, I found a vellum-bound copy of selected Browning, with lettering so ornate—gold lettering, black vellum—that it seemed to read, *R. Bnowning's Poetical Wonks*.

Mrs Shaw was staring at me. 'She's off her rocker,' I said, 'with the rocker busted into a million pieces. Talking to my grandmother's like drugs for free.'

Mrs Shaw turned back to the sink. She appeared unrelaxed.

I should have dried up, Mrs Shaw was washing up, but I couldn't face it. Instead I just sat down again at the table.

When she'd finished, I asked her whether she'd like another coffee.

She shrugged. She said, 'All right, actually no forget it.'

It was then that I asked her, almost light-headedly, 'What did you mean the other night by "fucking amateur"?'

Mrs Shaw leant against the sink edge, taking some of the weight off her feet, and dried her hands down her sides, then held them out, splayed, and looked at them for a moment. 'You don't want to hear this,' she said, as though to herself. 'You really don't want to hear this. Right, Micky's supposed to be going straight, right. We has to kick out of Bedford because of the meters. Utilities, right? Rooking meters? That's his thing, if you know what I mean, only keep it to yourself. Course he's been trying to figure out who's in it round here. Someone tells him some geezer round The Admiral does the black boxes. That's what we was doing in there when we meets *Constantine*—' she emphasised his name contemptuously, 'we was checking it out. So he's picking his pocket, and by bad luck he catches him, and what does he say? He only goes and says he won't say nothing if he'll learn him how to do it. So then he finds out what else he does, cards and that, credit cards, right, and he asks about it and that's the end of going straight. And you know what? Your *Constantine*, he's waiting to be done. He's watching for it, but he's bored out of his skull, like—like a kid; like tempted. He's up for it, like it's all new and he's *tempted*, you know? And they're making out like they're mates, but they ain't got no trust neither of them. And you know what? Bottom line, they're both bored, that's what, don't tell me. We just got chucked out this place we found, right, and I'm thinking we're going to have to doss it for the night. I don't even want to go in there. And guess what? There's your fucking amateur of a husband, and he tells us there's this, like, empty place downstairs of you two wanting repairs. He phones the landlord—landlord says we can have it temporary cut-price because he's been screwed by the bloke what's supposed to be fixing it up. Harbottle, what is it? Meets us in the pub. So that's us, suitcase each, load of bloody mould on the walls, and your *Constantine* upstairs bored out of his skull. I've got to go.' Mrs Shaw pushed forwards, taking the weight back onto her feet, and put her hand in her pocket. 'Screw it. Must've left the keys downstairs. Five minutes, you got a card I can borrow to open my door?'

Who knows quite what look passed over my face.

'Cheer up,' she said lazily. 'Joked you. You're all right.' And she held out her keys and cackled.

~

The pigeons opposite have gone again, ditto the man in the white plastic chair. It must be hazardous to sit plumb underneath the pigeons, but it's a sociable spot regardless. The minicab drivers drink there, argue, listen to the cricket, stand up to rehearse the odd dance move, laugh at each other.

After Mrs Shaw left, I brought the pink blanket back upstairs, sat down to organise my notes for work, failed to organise my notes for work and had a bath, which only slowly alleviated the fear that had got into me.

Con was allowing himself to be drawn into credit card fraud by someone who had tried to pick his pocket—and *failed*? Con was that disenchanted?—fatalistic?—tired? I remembered having read that when cars were first invented, many people assumed that no one would ever again walk the streets who had a pocket worth picking. It was kind of a response too far, when they thought about how things would be.

Forget Con, I said to myself. Be grateful you have work to do.

I *was* grateful, in fact—at least I was as I lay in the bath.

Plus, be happy about the imminent deadline attached to it, I thought, that'll keep you focussed. 'Deadline'—go back a century or more, and the term 'dead-line' refers to the marked limit around a prison beyond which an escaping convict can be shot.

Stop twatting about, I said to myself. I lay in the comforting water and tried to concentrate on how best I could use my time at the library. I planned to go there and lose myself in research, and in the words and cheap sentiments of my commission. I didn't want another whole day with my mind revolving on all the offensive bits and pieces of Con's spiel; nor, indeed, did I fancy the prospect of being plagued by Mrs Shaw's unassimilable news.

Nevertheless, as I lay there I did wonder why I was ready to believe her that Con might want to play fast and loose with the law. Well, but then I myself used to feel liberated by his occasional slips—slips?—occasional ardent, unheralded freaks of behaviour. I could see what Mrs Shaw was saying, although I don't know really that he's been 'bored out of his skull', as she put it. I would say more that he sounded desperate when he left me. But given that Mrs Shaw's picture of him is a fragmentary one, I suppose it fits well enough to think of him as bored—or at least, it doesn't not fit.

Work, I thought, go and lose yourself at the library: *work*. That was the plan, and so I'm all the more embarrassed by what actually happened.

'Deadline' brings back to me how Alphonso Ramble, my father's father, Stella Ramble's husband, killed a little old lady somewhat before she was due to die. Of course he wasn't really called Alphonso, but it doesn't matter.

I infer from the evidence available to me that Stella Ramble was the person in the world who made Alphonso happiest and unhappiest. I only once remember them holding hands, when their cat, Bingo, died in a traffic accident of which he was generally thought to have been the cause.

Alphonso was a doctor, and we're talking pre-NHS in the early part of his career. You billed the gentry and relied on their money, and they gave you pheasants, port and so on as well—and this was just about enough to allow you to wink at those who could only afford a cabbage or an egg. *I think perhaps you dropped—*

Alphonso had a seat set aside for him at the local flea pit so that, if Stella Ramble telephoned to say he was needed, the usherettes could fetch him out directly; and he'd be allowed to return to his seat a day or two later, for nothing, whenever he could fit it in, to watch the remainder of the film. He once saw a Marlene Dietrich movie in two halves when a lady patient wanted him at her house urgently, because, it turned out, she was worried about a sick pigeon.

This isn't anything to do with anything, but what was that pigeon suffering from, to warrant urgent action? Any number of possibilities spring to the informed mind: scissor beak, split eye, gout, bumble foot, canker, cancer, paratyphoid, tuberculosis, neuralgia, avian pox, measles, dementia, the jitters, divorce—who knows? Even an expert vet baulks at a request to determine the sicknesses of a feral pigeon. What hope for Alphonso?

One afternoon he went deep into the countryside, summoned by a farmer who had sent word of his old mother being ill. Near the end of the journey, the road became heavily rutted and muddy. Alphonso had to leave his car half a mile from the farm and walk. When he reached the house, he found the old woman sitting on a commode, surrounded by her five tall sons. That part of the world was referred to by country folk, perhaps still is referred to by real country folk, as 'boys' land', because it was unusually easy to work. So there stood five farmers, used to doing nicely.

'Let's move her onto the bed, shall we?' said Alphonso, opening his bag to get out his stethoscope.

'If you move her she'll die.' One of them said it but they all agreed: move her and she'd die.

Alphonso was annoyed and told them to move her, and because he was a doctor they did, and as they got her onto the bed, she died.

'I was frightened,' he told me. 'They were tall and there were five of them and my car was a mile away down the road, and let me tell you, I was pretty damn spooked.'

Alphonso liked to be prompted. Had I not asked what happened next, he wouldn't have carried on, so I asked.

He put his arm round me and gave me a little hug. 'I told them I'd known she was about to die, and that if she'd done it on the commode, there'd have had to be an inquest. I told them I'd got them to move her to avoid the necessity of proceedings, if you get my drift.'

'Did they believe you?' I asked.

'Thank God, *thank God*, they weren't sure.'

Alphonso, I have to say, was better at stories than jokes. It was sheer silliness that inclined him to repeat—so that I'll never forget it—the old line about the back-street dentist's advertising slogan: TEETH PULLED WHILE YOU WAIT.

So I went to the library, and it wasn't surprising that when I arrived, all the computers, which you're supposed to book, were being used. I hadn't thought to take reading material with me, and just sat there at one of the tables mucking about:

Bored of picking pockets? Tired of fiddling meters? Sick to death of rooking credit off other peoples cards? Thinking of getting away from life on earth? READ! NO! FURTHER! *For the ultimate escape try our special* Unlikely Adventures Magazine Special! Offer! Special! *If YOU have the guts for the ultimate not try the ultimate No-Go-Zone called SPACE? Shatter the original limits of YOUR dreams. We're not talking* REPRODUCTION *moon shit here. We,re talking* THE MOON *the moon. La* LUNA. *The thing you see at night. We,re talking one big ugly lump of rock reeling like a de-finned shark way out the next thing you get to after the sky has lost its nerve. From where YOU,RE sitting its only fifteen billion inches away. Were talking hostility of total freaking brain fucks the other side of a door. Out there getting inside YOUR! head. It,ll be YOU, YOUR prayers and destiny once the rocket fuel,s piss down a tube, eat dust and worry about sticking to the ceiling. YOU,RE too thick to fix the ship if the electrics crap out. But YOU! Can face it because YOU! ARE! REAL! MAN! and YOU read* Unlikely Adventures Magazine! *Smash your own nerve boundaries YOUR mental plate glass door. YOU! Send us fifty pence in Royal Mail stamps. WE! Send you all the specs a MAN needs to know. This is easy. Do not delay. Waiting gives you cancer. And CANCER! is the wrong way to die.*

I couldn't decide what to do with myself. This is a new problem for me which began on Saturday. For a while I did absolutely nothing. I sat at the library table and, against my will, eyed the library walls. The old stains and blotches were painted out a year ago in a refurbishment drive—no service for three weeks, two days and a morning—but now the marks are starting to show through again. I used to be fond of a compound stain above the crime shelves that looked like a rabbit, but it's only a glimmer so far. I'm waiting for the ears. *No ears.* I had the absurd sense that if I'd been able to resist looking, they would have been there.

When a computer came free, I first checked for emails and was pleased to find two. One was from some chap connected to Stella Ramble, who asked me whether she enjoyed being visited. The other was entitled 'Help!'

Dear Ramble,

I will confide the below to Professor Cohen before I send it, but please could you have another opinion about my English. I should like you to consider this letter as a confidential matter. Please could you delete this after you have told me your reply and I will delete also. Also one other question. How do you call the word that is opposite to 'anonymous'? Is this 'accredited'? How are you? Are you fine? I am truly. Many thanks already, Beata.

I by no means understood everything in the document she'd appended to this message, but that didn't necessarily prevent me helping Beata with her English.

On 3 Sept I was asked by the college to assess the worth of a bequest of c. 300 squeezes to be potentially donated to the college library by the widow of Mr Stephen Marfleet with also funding of £100 for purposes of cataloguing. I was requested to make this assessment as the only epigrapher in the college although my period is not the archaic. Marfleet's squeezes all appear to be from the archaic period and to be made on

Whatman filter paper 3 in the usual way. The fragments themselves are likely to be spolia or remains from sites disturbed by modern cultivation or likewise. It is my understanding that Mrs Marfleet is unable to supply accurate information on provenance. Consequently the value of Marfleet's squeezes is very little although to be accurate, I can say they are mostly taken of very small and uninterpretable fragments although one larger one appears to be written in false boustrophedon from the left and two are definitely retrograde. It is my understanding that Mrs Marfleet is willing to donate the remainder of the £100 to the library after work is completed cataloguing the squeezes. I believe it would be false pretences to accept this money as anything other than a gift to the library of £100. Albeit I am not entitled to ignore the possibility that an expert in this field might disagree, but it is my understanding that I am forbidden by college rules to consult any expert outside the college. The clear person to consult is Professor Cohen who could presently confirm or disconfirm my opinion with ease. It would have been reasonable if allowed by college rules for me to consult Professor Cohen, but as not, my recommendation is that the library board should consult Professor Cohen and then the college can prefer what outcome it desires.

Yours.

Though Beata's general meaning was clear at all times, the poor state of her English was a sign that she was both irritated and shaken. Off the bat, I sent her a few questions of my own. What is 'false boustrophedon'? What is, or are, 'spolia'? Most especially, what is 'a squeeze'? In reply to her questions—'How are you? Are you fine?'—I said I was fine.

At the time of saying this, lost in contemplation of her epi-graphical black hole, it was true.

I printed out a copy of her email to work on at home. Then I deleted.

For some minutes I sat motionless at the computer wondering why I hadn't myself said *Help!* to Beata. The best answer I came up with was David Curtis. She went out with him two years ago. He was a clever, darting sort of person, and had an overcoat that went down to his ankles, which I would have mentioned even if it hadn't been the coat that finished them off.

During a cold spell, she put her hand into one of its front pockets for comfort, only to find that it was split wide open along the inside seam. Here's a tender picture. Beata is cold and puts her hand into David Curtis's coat pocket. It's split. No! Both pockets are split! In an uncharacteristically domestic mood, she offers to sew them up again.

Here's what happens next. David Curtis informs her that his coat is more than just a coat. In certain bookshops—he's a Latinist—he has a habit of dropping a book or two into the pockets so that they fall through and down to the bottom, where he has perfectly competently attached the hem to the lining—using safety pins. It has come to him that, by this means, in these certain particular bookshops, any stolen items will travel out below the detector beams that set off the security alarm.

Beata protests. David Curtis insults her. Still she protests. Curtis retrenches and makes a big thing of how, as a matter of principle, he has never passed off as a gift, to anyone, a book he's acquired by theft. All the books he's ever given her, for example, have been *paid for*, though, admittedly, yes, this might, yes, have been accomplished using money he's made from selling books that he *has* stolen. He'd like to be sure, but, he's being honest now: he can't be sure.

Beata is discriminating. Undoubtedly the word 'discriminating' applies to Beata. And yet, with regard to David Curtis's nicety about how he has paid for her gifts, her powers of discrimination fail her.

So ends one more human liaison. Beata's opinion of English men shrivels.

I tried to pull myself together. It was imperative that I faff around on the Web. I needed good material on two more ice-carving festivals, and settled for looking at one in Alaska and one in China. I've been drawn to the one in China from the start.

The pictures I hit on were garish, with Palace-of-Westminster ice sculptures inexplicably popular around the world. According to a nameless hack who had taken this path before me, 'the neon illuminations make for a fun and fantasy filled spectacle at night but daylight proffers the natural energy planes within the carvings'.

I had a preliminary go at it myself. *For all the razzle-dazzle, there is something sad to knowing that these complex works are in a state of slow meltdown.*

I saw at once that this was no good. *Meltdown* read all wrong, restored to its literal meaning; plus *slow* was questionable. I thought: probably an ice sculpture wouldn't melt at all during the sub-zero periods chosen for the festivals. I also asked myself, what would be sad about it if they *did* melt?

I get anxious about issues like this when I'm working on

a piece, and then remember that what I say matters not in the slightest. Anyway, I was doing better than the person who'd written, 'which showstopper vision will embed itself in your memory with effortless ease'. I jotted this down in my notebook on the thought that I might amuse myself by infiltrating it into one of my own future articles.

I had hardly begun to work when I was disturbed. A man took over the computer on my deaf side, but ignored his own screen and instead looked back and forth between me and mine. Under this degree of scrutiny, I felt ashamed of what I was doing, and wrote, *Amongst the more highly educated people on the planet, only those snobs who are kitsch-loving bottom-feeders of the worst order could possibly find these ice carvings attractive.*

I understand that people stare at me when I'm walking along the street, but I was moving only my eyes and fingers. I couldn't bear my neighbour's attention. Ineptly, I admit, without thought, and—unable to make myself look and check—vaguely afraid that we might somehow be acquainted, I tumbled out the question, 'Who are you?'

He snorted as he replied, 'I'm fine, thank you.'

Perhaps he was off his head. Perhaps he was yet deafer than I am. I grabbed my notebook and pencil, shoved them into my pocket while hoiking myself to my feet, swiped my bag up and left, which, besides any other consideration, means I'll have to get back again tomorrow.

Con, in his speech, said furiously, 'If you didn't have to go out and get email and look up junk on the Web, I don't think you'd go out full stop.' He was exaggerating, but this has been his perpetual explanation for why I can't be wired up at home.

What do I mean, *can't*? I know: somehow it's more possible to think about these questions now he isn't here.

Each time since Saturday lunch that the phone has rung, or there has been a message waiting, I've felt frightened it'll be Con, though each time I've found myself hoping I'm about to discover where he is. We are still married, in a way.

The phone went again today as I got back from my curtailed library trip. I waited five rings before I answered: Johnson.

'Look, Ramble, what's going on?'

'Oh, hi.' I swapped the phone to my good ear. 'How's things? Yes, oh, well, hi, I'm still stuck,' I managed to slow down, 'still stuck on these terrible ice sculptures. I'm still looking at a Chinese one, "the Moscow of the Orient", what does *that* phrase summon up? I've taken notes on it twice but I can't decide if it'll do me, and I haven't even finished writing up the Yuki Matsuri festival yet, which will have to work—it gets two million visitors a year, incredibly. Do I mean that? It—you know—Johnson, this whole ice-carving business, I don't know, I don't have time to change tack.' The next thing I said was, 'I mean, you'd have to be a seriously unrepentant cultural bottom-feeder to like anything about it.'

An acid laugh came down the line. 'I object to you using "bottom-feeder" as a term of abuse, and not because my name is Pike.'

'Blimey, Johnson, keep a lid on it!'

'Oh yes?' he said silkily. 'Why?'

'Hey Johnson, I was thinking in bed last night—' I was rescued from conversational breakdown at this point by a tiny detail in the back of my mind: 'in bed last night' was just me playing for time, '—surely you were supposed to have had a big inheritance for being landed with such a loopy name?'

'Well remembered.' Johnson sounded as brittle as I felt.

'I think that was practically the first thing you ever told me about yourself, on the metal bench at my father's.'

'Yes, no,' he sighed, 'you're right. Dad used to claim it would get us money out of his godfather. Whether it's supposed to come to Dad or to me I don't know, I don't think he was very clear about it, Johnny Johnson. He hasn't died yet. But I reckon it was probably just sucking up on Dad's part blah blah blah. I don't suppose there's genuinely any agreement. But how about this? I only recently found out, you'll like this, "John Johnson" was the preferred alias of—' he paused dramatically, 'Guy Fawkes!'

'Oh superb,' I said, and meant it. 'Wow, this all begins to sounds like a bit of low-grade Victorian plotting, i.e. slack and yet contorted.'

'Your call.'

'It's strange—' I paused to think what I intended to say, but only properly worked it out as I spoke, 'how we come up with all these weird ideas for linking ourselves to each other, and yet everybody's lonely really.'

'Are you lonely, darling?' Johnson's way of saying 'darling' isn't in the least soft, but his question was a throwaway even so. He wasn't any longer trying to push me with, 'Look, what's going on?'

'Lonely? Yes. How about you?'

'Yes,' said Johnson. 'I'm lonely. Definitely I am. It's a fucker. It's bad. It's *germs*.'

'Honestly Johnson, how old are you? Nine?'

'Yes, I am, basically. I'm about nine. Ramble, listen, I'm in the bookshop the next couple of days, but listen, I'll call you on Thursday, okay? Deal?'

'Deal.'

'Check,' he said, like a secret-service agent.

It was almost funny, his opening wish to make me talk, versus my shapeless fear of what might happen if I did. It isn't that I don't trust Johnson. I trust him the most of anybody.

So I was left with the promise of another phone call. We'd said 'deal'. This means he will definitely call me on Thursday.

'Oh no!' I shouted. 'Oh no!' I grabbed the phone back to my ear, but he had already rung off.

What if the man in the library hadn't been saying, 'I'm fine, thank you,' but had had some cosmopolitan name like, 'Ifan Thangu'?

Privately, I blushed.

Beata lived in the next room down the corridor from me when I was in my second year at university. Life seems agreeable after all when I consider that I was able to make a friend I like as much as her simply by finding her next door. She was reading Classics then. Later she did a PhD on a type of Byzantine praise literature, the obscure canon of which, across several centuries, is made up of a set of enormously long and fantastically boring orations.

Whatever question she started out intending to answer, it ended up as the following. How was it bearable for so many people to put so much sophisticated effort into a form of writing so dull?

I imagine that when things got rough, she must have asked

herself a similar question with regard to her own endeavours. All the same, it doesn't take much to see how interesting her enquiry really was. BRIDE EATEN BY ALLIGATOR will surely always qualify in the minds of a significant number of people as a story worth telling, but how do you perpetuate, across generations of Byzantine individuals, a taste for undiluted literary tedium?

~

After my uneasy conversation with Johnson—the second of its kind in as many days, I realised with a sinking heart—I came upstairs to work on my ice piece; but again I couldn't bring myself even to re-read my notes. Instead I drifted into tidying up Beata's Marfleet letter, which took nearly half an hour.

Still no pigeons. I kept glancing up, I'm not sure why, habit I guess. 'Are you lonely, darling?' *No pigeons.* I sat and occupied myself writing until the light began to wane: *he sounded desperate when he left me, Poetical Wonks,* TEETH PULLED WHILE YOU WAIT, *Help!,* REPRODUCTION *moon shit, undiluted literary tedium.*

When, finally, the day began to ebb, I gave up in an instant, just suddenly went downstairs and slouched on the sofa. I thought about television but didn't turn it on because I'd already closed my eyes in an attempt to ward off a thin kind of dread. Yes, but don't worry about that, I said to myself, you're in shock, right?

With nightfall itself, I was fleetingly aware that time had passed. I stayed put though, and after a while, tipped over sideways, rested my head on the left sofa arm, and, without exactly meaning to, fell deeply asleep.

I was woken by the sound of someone thumping at the door. The room was dark apart from the orange street light cast up through the lime leaves making blurs on the ceiling. I didn't imagine it was Con. I understood that it was Mrs Shaw, drunk, or perhaps still avoiding her husband.

My mouth was parched and I had a headache, but this was nothing to the burning pain in my pelvis as I straightened up and rose to my feet. I was barely able make it to the door, where, without preamble, Mrs Shaw exploded: 'I'm so fucking stupid. Put the light on, okay. Do you read your meter? I cannot believe I was telling you this morning and I didn't even click.'

'Sometimes,' I whispered, trying to swallow. 'Sometimes Mr Harbottle does it.'

'Fuck. I was about to go to bed and I thought.'

'What's the matter?' I could only just speak. I put on the entrance light and flinched.

'Your fucking husband wanted to be taught the game on everything. He was all bloody questions, like a kid, bloody idiot. No way he wouldn't have wanted his meter fixed.'

'What?'

She addressed me slowly, as though she had worked out I was a retard. 'Where's your meter? *Electrics*. Where's your *meter*?'

I gestured to where it is, in the cupboard under the stretch of internal staircase that leads to the top floor.

It was difficult for her to see. I had no torch to offer her, and didn't think I could make it to the kitchen for a candle.

I slopped against the coats hanging behind me and tried to steady myself.

Mrs Shaw bent into the cupboard and I heard her cloistered voice saying, 'Fucking prick.'

She'd put a small canvas bag on the floor, open, with tools in. She had also brought up a hairdryer.

'All the bloody dust's got marks in,' she said, pulling back out again. 'Anyone can see.'

She grabbed a screwdriver and set to work in the cupboard. I dragged slowly along the walls back to the sofa, and sat there with my head in my hands. I desperately wanted a drink of water, but not so much that I could face getting myself all the way to the kitchen.

I'm not sure how long it took Mrs Shaw to finish. She came up to me dishevelled. 'You're going to have to wipe it down tomorrow and put the dust back natural. Can't do it in the dark.'

I didn't respond.

'Right girl,' she said, 'put you on the safe side, you need to put your heaters on, your cooker, your lights, your music, whatever you've got. I brought my hairdryer up. Lucky the weather's been like this, overnight should do you. Leave it all on overnight, numbers go up normal and you're golden, right? Bedford way, we call it hot-housing.'

I recoiled again as she jabbed on the overhead light. I suppose I looked confused. I was confused. I sat there, confused.

'All right then,' she said crossly.

When she'd turned on every possible light and appliance

in the kitchen, she came back through, still angry. 'You listen to me,' she said. 'You don't want that Harbottle on your case. He's a nasty fucking piece of fucking shit. He figures out your numbers don't stack up, he'll have you out of here like that. Or worse, you hear?'

'Worse?'

She took a steely breath and turned away. She switched on everything she could in the main room, barring Con's electric keyboard, which instinct must have warned her to avoid. Then she disappeared upstairs.

With impressive speed the flat became unbearable. All three bars on the fire glowed, I presume the oven was on too, and every light bulb blazed. Water, I guess hot, poured noisily from the taps in the kitchen and the bathroom, and drained noisily away again through the exposed pipe work. The hairdryer roared, the TV showed a late-night fight flick, the World Service came on on the radio next to the bed upstairs. In the room with me, a Charlie Parker CD struggled in the tide. The volume of noise made my deaf ear throb. I had to screw up my eyes against the 100-watt glare, and I was flushed with the heat, though pain was making me shiver.

Mrs Shaw rematerialised. 'Come on,' she said. By now I was having to lip-read. I think she considered grabbing my arm with her free hand. With the other she was managing her bag of tools, and also one of our pillows and the pink blanket. Once again she used her retard manner. 'You've had your meter running *backwards*, right? Harbottle's over tomorrow. You're going to have to spend the night down mine. If Micky gets in, we'll just deal.'

I had a nonsensical desire to explain to her—as Con, at

the keyboard, had once explained to me—how Charlie Parker had been a fan of Ravel.

The way I'd fallen asleep on the sofa, bent over sideways, my pelvic ligament had pulled askew. A mistake like this is serious for me. I could only manage the stairs sitting down. I had to move my legs one by one—pick them up by hand; shift them ahead of the rest of me a step at a time; lift my body down after with the strength in my arms; shift each leg down; lift my body down. Mrs Shaw stopped and looked back through the banisters at me, unselfconsciously repelled.

I found myself muttering, 'It's rude to stare.' My mind circled this phrase as I mulled over the fact that, while I do have crutches, they happened to be up in a corner in the bedroom. I was certain Mrs Shaw would dislike having to fetch them if this required her to press past a cripple.

Yes, I thought, Madame Tussaud's: *it's rude to stare.*

Mrs Shaw disappeared down below. I didn't immediately process that she'd said, 'Screw it. I'll catch you in a minute.'

With each of the tight bends in the staircase, the horrible muddle of noise above me became less audible. The angled steps were more awkward and painful to manage than the straight ones, so my sense of the volume of sound reduced in jerks.

By the time I'd got myself to the open door of Mrs Shaw's flat, I was not able to focus well on ordinary things, though I did take in that the near-empty room before me was so devoid of Bobbo Stothard's effect that it was incredible to think she'd been living there only three weeks earlier. Bobbo was keen on coverlets, tablecloths, antimacassars &c. Instead of floral curtains with matching pelmet, there was now a fog-coloured dust sheet wedged in over the rail.

Mrs Shaw pointed at the sofa. Exposed in its original, ugly fabric, it was not unlike ours. My pillow and blanket were already laid out on it with military neatness.

I loitered in the doorway, mutely gathering the strength of will to make it to my sleeping place; then, without a wall to lean on, I began.

Somehow I got there. When I lay down I closed my eyes. I understood from the sounds that Mrs Shaw was pulling up the plywood coffee table, and that she sat herself on it right beside me. I wondered whether this was really how she'd spent Friday night.

'You okay?'

'Yes.'

'You want something? Call the doctor's for you if you give me a number.'

'No.'

'Right then.' She stood up again.

'Do you know where they've gone?' I asked.

There was a long pause.

'Thing is,' she said at last, 'no—you're better off keeping well out. Don't know, can't tell—if you don't, I mean. That way, if there's trouble, like, don't know, can't tell: you've kept your story straight, because—you don't have one, right? You need the toilet? It's upstairs.'

'I know.' I opened my eyes to look at her, but saw nothing in her that I could interpret. I felt my heart race. 'What trouble?' I whispered. 'If there's what sort of trouble?'

She sighed. She sighed at *me*. 'All right, you asked, don't blame me, you asked, right? You want to know, I'll tell you. Micky, right, he says he'll show him whatever he likes if he helps him with a credit card Saturday afternoon. Micky's into it by now. Micky, right, he looks like what he is, he looks like the streets. But he was took by your *Constantine*. "Ho ho, this one'll make a flash grafter," you know? That's what he says to me: "What won't I do with this one!" So, Saturday afternoon, that's it, they was off out going to rinse it. And off they goes, and they ain't come back, and that's all I can tell you.'

'It was arranged for Saturday?'

'Yes. Friend of Micky's had him lined up for a card.'

'For Saturday? In advance? It was arranged?'

'Yes.'

I deferred considering this too closely. 'What's rinsing— did you say "rinsing" it?'

'There's ways and ways,' said Mrs Shaw. 'Depends who you're dealing with.'

'So my, he, they—but they did—Saturday, they went and did this?'

'Don't know,' she said. 'Who gives a fuck by now? They're not here are they?'

I knew how far it was from the flat door to where I lay. To most people, not far. 'You really think your husband's coming back?' I asked.

'Will he come back? You mean, will he *ever*?' She laughed. 'He'll be back. If he's on a bender he's got this tart he sees in Brighton, don't think I don't know. Could be a while. Hey,' she said, 'here's us worrying about a couple of wankers, why *do* we bother? They'll be back.'

'I don't know,' I whispered. I had to shut my eyes again. In this condition of semi-darkness, I heard myself tell her, 'My husband said he was leaving me. I mean he said it like he meant it.'

There was a plastic rustling noise in one corner as Mrs Shaw mumbled, 'Better hope you're wrong.'

'Why?'

'Why?' she said.

I felt all of a sudden close to a kind of dead sleep. My voice came out spectrally thin. 'I don't know. I'm beginning to consider whether—whether I actually, you know, *like* him even. He's so—the thing is, he's so difficult. I've been sort of thinking that I partly married him just for the ridiculous reason that he was certain about it.'

'Well,' she said brusquely, 'don't push your luck.'

The room had only a single, low-wattage light bulb, but even with my eyes shut I registered the abrupt increase in dimness as Mrs Shaw switched it off. I heard her go through her kitchen and start up the stairs. 'Everyone's difficult, you know?' she was saying. 'Everyone's difficult.' Her voice carried down through the maisonette, milder, further away. 'I mean, he leaves you for real, girl, legs like that, you're shafted.'

4

Tuesday

I woke up in a pool of dulled light. The air was still, and sweet, laced with a damp smell I hadn't noticed previously. I liked lying there at street level with footsteps on the pavement immediately outside. I wondered who would be walking in our neighbourhood at dawn, if it was dawn. There was little sound of traffic, and only this solitary passer-by.

I thought about shifting myself, but understood that it would hurt. Just as I was, I felt no particular excess of pain. I stared at the strip of light under the flat door and imagined Mr Shaw coming in: the sound of a key in the building lock, then one in the flat door lock, the door swinging open, Mr Shaw slouching in. Briefly, my heart yammered; but in the peacefulness of simply lying there, huddled on the sofa, I calmed right down again and fell back asleep.

The second time I came to, Mrs Shaw was pulling the dust sheet down from the curtain rail. The room remained shadowy. I realised what a blessing it is that on the top floor we catch the morning sun.

'You in there?' she said.

I was.

As I manoeuvred myself up into a sitting position I was hit by a wave of nausea, but it soon passed. It wasn't too bad.

Mrs Shaw looked me over. 'Any better?' she asked.

'I am better.' I took a deep breath and then stuttered over it breathing in doubly so that my lungs were too full as I remembered what awaited me upstairs. Had it really been necessary to turn everything on full all night?

'Would it be—' I rocked to test my pain margins, 'could I ask you a favour?'

'I don't mind.'

I hesitated to put her to any trouble, even though—well, I don't know what. 'Might I ask you to go,' I caught my breath again, winced, 'to go and fetch out this brace thing from the top left-hand drawer in the bedroom, it's a kind of, it's a—' I described it to her until she made a disgusted sound in the back of her throat, '—it's a whitish, massive piece of elastic, this wide, with palm-sized squares of Velcro at either end. You can't miss it. It's something you put round you like this when—'

'Euelgh,' said Mrs Shaw.

I would have liked to be able to explain that only abject necessity was inducing me to direct, to my underwear drawer, someone with her sheeny sense of style. I wondered whether the brace was yet infused with the perfume of the *Blomchet* soaps.

'Is it too much to ask?'

'Course not,' she said. 'Here, fetch us your pillow and blanket.'

*

I prayed that while she was up there she would turn off all the taps, switches and machines that she had previously seen fit to turn on. I wasn't so worried about the lights, nor about a build-up of heat, but I did fear having to wade through a barrage of noise.

My father used to complain endlessly about noise: fridges, aeroplanes, computers, car horns, hot water pipes, cold water pipes, ice cream vans, &c. &c. The only thing he never heard was my mother's off-red Roberts Dynatron radio.

He would sit at the piano for hours, supposedly running through repertoire, so-to-speak practising; but mostly improvising—he was an obsessive improviser—usually his own, fraught, semi-dissonant, keyboard-wide jazz. Improvising was how he talked to himself, so it seemed, or to the other musicians whose solos he invoked with maniac fingers; while she— this was a part of my upbringing—listened to trashy crooners, top volume, all around the house.

The two of them tried to blank each other out. I had to listen to both at once. I could name, and it would take quite a long time, all my mother's favourite songs; the ones she thrills to, the ones she merely endures, not to mention the ones that make her change station. With my father it was more subtle, whether he sounded loose, or frustrated, or *happy*. Their cacophony, disentangled and interpreted, was a close indicator of their moods. In my early childhood, if the noise wasn't right, I would droop on my bed, immobilised.

About a year ago, Con started to compose through headphones. It isn't possible to get an upright into our flat, the staircase is too narrow, so he has—we have—only an electric keyboard. He told me Bobbo Stothard had made some comment about his music. He'd become concerned, he said, that he was being a nuisance. It's a line of his, 'I don't want to disturb anybody'; except that, from the start, not hearing what he was up to disturbed me greatly.

When there's a panic on with a job, Con sometimes writes at Uncle Joe's place: his boss's place. There, presumably, Con composes out loud. But this past year, when he's been working at home, all I've had to go on has been the creepy, padded clicking of the keys.

Mrs Shaw strode back into her flat with a businesslike air. I struggled to my feet feeling faint. She handed me my brace at arm's length, letting go so promptly that I almost fumbled receiving it. She pointed at my legs with her hairdryer, I suppose to acknowledge that I was standing on them, and said, 'Less worse than you was, anyway.'

'I will be now.'

Normally I would put the brace on underneath a loose dress or skirt, but I strapped it over my clothes, as tight as possible, feeling horribly watched, though I was relieved to be bound in its grip. As I managed this, my mind volunteered the caption: 'What need to strive with a life awry?'

'You know, don't forget to sort out your meter,' said Mrs Shaw.

'Sorry, how, I don't—?' Facetiously, I was thinking, not *my* metre, Browning's!

> Fail I alone, in words and deeds?
> Why all men strive, and who succeeds?

'I—sorry,' I said. 'How do I do that? I mean—'

She interrupted, 'So get the dust off of something else, right, spray a bit of hairspray on like this, for glue, right,' she mimed the act of spraying, 'and then just—' Mrs Shaw held her hands out and made her fingertips quiver sprinklingly.

Something about this performance left me defeated. I mimed her mime back at her.

'Pardon me saying,' she didn't quite smile, 'but you ain't got no hairspray, right?'

'Given the state of my hair?'

This rejoinder was completely unnecessary. We both knew she meant: given the state of my hair.

'Jish,' said Mrs Shaw, and disappeared up to her bathroom.

Jish?

The morning felt as though it was going badly. I had enough reasons to be downhearted, I'd say, but by this stage I was feeling depressed at the morning in itself. I felt, standing there, that I was ready to go to bed, for hours, not that I'd only just got up. And I didn't want to be standing. I hate standing. I wavered on my feet. Crossly I reflected that, myself, if I had run away from Bedford with one suitcase, I would not have packed hairspray, a hairdryer and three pairs of high-heeled shoes; although, if I'd run away from *Bedford*, who knows?

Mrs Shaw handed me the can in a perfectly normal manner. 'I'd offer you to keep it,' she said, and this time she did smile.

I said, 'You should meet my mother.'

From the noise she made in reply, I rather took it that Mrs Shaw had difficulty imagining I'd got one.

'I didn't say,' she closed her eyes, 'but when you've done putting the dust on, right, you'll be wanting to blow off the extra,'—then opened them. 'It's okay,' she said. 'Do it as best as you can. I can always check it for you. You should eat, right.'

I had to run this last comment through my head twice before I grasped that, with the brace on, she could see how pinched and meagre I am inside my unfitted summer clothing.

My own meagreness was yet another subject to fill me with gloom, and I must have lost concentration over it, because some spiralling line of thought jarred when Mrs Shaw said, 'I'm not being funny, but, like, you better get out of here, you know?'

Not only was she agitated, she had been from the moment she'd woken me up. It wasn't until this point—what a fool I am—that I understood it. She wanted me out of her flat.

'I'm not being funny.' How about rude? I couldn't help thinking this: well, if not funny, how about rude?—but I also felt unnerved. It was an upsetting novelty to see her like this.

I left at once, omitted to say thanks, and got myself, with rest stops, up the stairs.

I didn't shut the door to her flat behind me, but she did. I heard her do it when I was three flights up. As I climbed the top flight, that leads to my own door, my spirits rose. I could hear that there was no talk radio, no CD on ceaseless replay, no daytime television, no draining water. I walked in. She'd dealt with everything. The only noise was traffic from the street, which sounded closer than usual through the wide-open windows. She had even pushed the windows right up for me. The air was fuggy to a degree that made breathing unpleasant, but there was a breeze outside, sufficiently strong for me to hear the lime leaves shallying on their stalks. The air would cool.

Trees these days, in England, hold on to their foliage for

longer than ever; and when the first real drop happens, often many more leaves fall in one go than used to be the case, sometimes as many as three quarters of them. A strong wind without rain, causing a late, heavy, city-wide leaf drop, is the municipal street-sweeper's idea of an extremely bad thing. Leaves are far easier to pick up wet than dry. A mass drop of dry leaves is backbreaking work for the person detailed to remove them. England is getting warmer and the trees don't have the same timetables any more. I know this because last autumn I asked a street-sweeper why he was swearing at a tree.

What would Mrs Shaw have been thinking as she went through my flat? It's drab, I admit. I'm not sure why we haven't done more to improve it, to make the place look welcoming, except that we never meant to stay.

I should have taken some of Stella Ramble's things when I emptied out her house. She had a lot of wrecked antiques: furniture with the veneer split by decades of central heating; fly-flecked Victorian embroideries; chipped botanical oils reverse-painted on glass, and so on. I found her tailor's dummy was gone, but didn't notice that anything else was missing. I took the sea-green velvet cushion, on a whim, plus a box of photographs and documents, the copy of R. *Bnowning's Poetical Wonks* and a 1928 book about Berlin; nothing much else.

I hadn't been clear what I was supposed to do with all her possessions. When I found out Gander Ramble was a signatory to her will, I was able to ask him whether he knew what the rules were. I didn't want to approach her solicitor, I preferred to operate without knowing the legal view of the question, but I did ask Gander Ramble whether there were specific items she had left to people, and if so, whether these items could be given out straight away, or needed to be kept somewhere, in effect to be nursed themselves, until she finally died.

His reply left me fraught with a sense that Stella Ramble had wrapped up her affairs with one foot behind her in the lost world of horses.

'It's a shame the way people want to grub about in wills in advance,' he said. 'They might just wait until it's actually curtains. But I must say, your grandmother's is pretty awful. I think you'll find the Mothers' Union and some two-bit outfit called Pelham Merrit's sop up just about the lot of it. Her bloody man—what's he called?—didn't say a word to her about you, I'll warrant. And if he did it didn't hit home. I should take anything you like, although I expect they'll have an eye out for the silver and jewellery. They'll be listed on the insurance, you know. What's he called? Hopp. Hopp will want the contents revalued at sale prices if they haven't been already, and frankly, it'll do him out of a bob or two if you organise the selling yourself. Don't let him do it. You do it. He'll bank the cash, and he'll want the paperwork by the way; and if there's anything left when she dies, it'll go to the Mothers' Union.'

I was in a dark frame of mind back then for all sorts of reasons, including the fact that my stepmother, Elise, was refusing to help me on the grounds that at my father's funeral, Stella Ramble had declined to understand who Elise was. There was a great deal of labour involved, but Con had deadlines; and my mother certainly wasn't interested.

Stella Ramble's house contents, in detail, were peculiar. It transpired that she'd had a fetish for scissors, owned thirty-seven pairs. And she'd kept an old suitcase that was jam-packed with handkerchiefs; this despite the fact that, a while after Alphonso died, she'd moved in from the country and had shed something like two thirds of their possessions.

Anyway, the upshot of my sorting was that I sold, gave away, donated to charity shops or destroyed absolutely everything barring *Bnowning's Wonks*, &c.

Beata, who is multi-lingual, translated for me an inscription scribbled on the title page of the Berlin book: '*Zur Erinnerung an Berlin! von Papa*', meaning, 'To help you remember Berlin! from *Papa*'. It was dated 26.6.29. This raised questions that the book itself didn't answer.

After my conversation with Gander Ramble I checked out Pelham Merrit's. It came over as being something like a mutant survivor of the old Distressed Gentlewomen's associations. I have thought since that I should myself apply. If my grandmother is a gentlewoman, am I not one also? The answer to that is, *obviously not*, distressed or otherwise; but I don't know why not. I think of the way Stella Ramble has lived, let alone my mother, and I think of the way I live, and I can't quite work out why the difference is so enormous.

In the old days when I visited my grandmother, before she went inside, she would always give me what she called 'a dab in the hand'—whatever she found in her purse, five pounds, ten pounds. She didn't understand the worth of these sums to me. She had always had more than enough. Five pounds, ten pounds; it didn't mean a thing to her.

At first I minded the knowledge that she hadn't remembered me in her will, but I asked myself: why should that money come to me? It was earned through the toxic drudgery of workers in a Victorian wallpaper factory in Leeds. Why should it come to me?

I'm days late visiting Stella Ramble. I should phone her but I can't face it. After my embarrassing exit from the library yesterday, I need to go back again, now, and I haven't the strength to do her as well.

Tomorrow, perhaps.

I have the sense that I am deferring everything that's important.

Enough writing. Now I have to go.

~

I decided to set out there and then before I gave up. I had to use my crutches. They're conspicuous, but in a way preferable to gimping it, if you even have a choice. With crutches, strangers assume you've had an accident and are going to get better. This makes you less interesting than a bona fide cripple. Another good thing about crutches is that you can use them to whack aside junk mail, as I did when I reached the front door.

I swung along the High Street, entertainingly fast from my perspective; busy about my day, really, though lost inside my head:

Thinking of getting away from your tedious WIFE? You can, you should, and you will! Antidotal evidence reveals that most marriages excels people's lowest expectations a much amount more than realised. But why hark on your troubles? The expenses occurred in terms of waste cannot be underestimated.

Remedialwise, give HER! the short shift treatment NOW! and in a few days hence you will be beholding to no one: a law onto yourself. Oh yes! Women: resplendent in their diversity! Remember the last recent few you've genuinely wanted? Enjoy their lack of scruples. Exploit their own glass ceilings. Flatter them and it's guaranteed they'll want to flatter you! In due course of time, then more and more increasingly! Does she beleaguer on about her little problems? WIVES all do! Who needs another half? Half? is surrendering too much. Half? is shooting yourself in the shins. Half? is spastic reasoning from earlier times of yore. Womankind: caked in mystery! It's a learning curb! Quit while you're ahead! So you married a cripple and you can't make her run away? No problem! Run away yourself! So you got stuck with an AUTISTIC VAMPIRE? So what? Time to take control of—

I knew I knew something about vampires. Edward Lloyd, in 1845 if I'm getting this right, published the first, the original, the *pilot* vampire text of English literature, *Varney*. So what? Only that I knew I knew more about vampires.

Like an automaton, I swung my way along the High Street and in through the glass doors of the library. They were wedged wide open. I only got a grip on myself when I saw, out of the corner of my eye, that, on the inside of one of them, on the back of a notice intended to be read from the front, someone had scribbled in pencil: 'check out the skirt'.

Ifan Thangu, to my relief, wasn't anywhere to be seen. *Make your own fucking friends.* Oh sure—Ifan Thangu?

Before I got to work, I sent Beata my version of her Marfleet letter. It's stupid that I had to carry a corrected print-out from home back to the library, and then had to re-type it into a computer there in order to send it as an email; but this is how I do things.

I looked in my notebook and decided to jettison material I had scrabblingly gathered on Manchu ice lanterns. 'Jetsam' is a corruption of 'jettison'. The two were interchangeable until marine insurers decided to ascribe them distinct meanings. It doesn't matter.

Manchu ice lanterns, what a waste of time. What I needed, still, was an entire third ice festival. I started to trawl the Web. Quebec? St Petersburg? Indoors somewhere in Holland? Indoors?—forget it. Alaska? Alaska? Alaska? I had thousands of sites at my disposal, it was a question of picking something.

I sat in our one-room, backwater library, and did for an hour what is called, in business speak, 'environmental scanning'. This term happens also to be a euphemism for commercial espionage. So, I environmentally scanned, I took notes, and my mind wandered, but I was working.

I was taking notes and my mind was wandering and I found myself thinking about what Mrs Shaw had said. First, that I must be sure to fix my meter. Second, that Mr Harbottle would be coming round today. Mr Harbottle? I staggered to my feet. Christ, I thought, I haven't done the meter. *Christ Almighty. I'm about to get evicted.*

All the way home I talked furiously to myself about dust. My mind narrowed down to this single topic—I was cocooned by pain, and by the rhythm of swinging on my crutches. How much did I need and where would I get enough?

There was dust all over the flat—but to get enough? I could only think of the top of the kitchen cupboards; but to reach that high would involve climbing on a chair, which would be dangerous for me to attempt, let alone succeed at; the sort of circumstance in which I might, without warning, fold, and, not fully balanced, fall. I can't allow myself to fall. In short, the only thing I could think was: you're shafted.

You waste time in your life minding that your flat is dirty, then when you need a bit of dust, you can't reach.

I knew I was being unclear through panic. Another place for dust, another place for dust, would be within the meter cupboard itself. But surely, wouldn't that be too obvious?

I skipped going to the Minimart. That was another unclear piece of thinking. Bread, soup, milk, something, I needed supplies.

My mind kept coming back to the same difficulty, that I was going to have to ask Mrs Shaw to sweep off the tops of the kitchen cupboards for me, possibly worse, or even actually worse, than getting her to poke about in my underwear drawer.

I let myself into our building. Through her door I could hear that she was in so I knocked—regretting it as I did so. I'd asked too much of her already.

She took a strangely long time. As I waited, calming down, sort of calming down, my mind slid back to my work. I stared at my feet. Would I be able to get away with having aborted this latest library visit? I had a fair whack of material now. Perhaps I should use floating Manchu ice lanterns after all? *Nice pictures*, very, but not quite right for the piece, though why not? What was the problem? 'Manchu ice lanterns' sounds lovely; Sax Rohmer: *Fu Manchu*—

Mrs Shaw's door swung open. I was unnerved by a diffuse feeling of mortification, and sounded all jumpy to myself as I said, 'Could I ask for your help a minute?'

Her loaded silence caused me to raise my head. When I'm talking to someone I can hear, I try at least to make myself look, if not properly at them, then only slightly past them. I looked slightly past Mrs Shaw into her flat. Eye to eye, appallingly, I encountered Mr Harbottle. I dropped my gaze again at once. 'Sorry,' I croaked. With my crutches at angles like walking sticks, I stepped away. 'Sorry.'

But why was I apologising? There was something wrong. Not *nice pictures*. Why not, though? I stared at the floor. I couldn't reconstruct what I'd seen, what was still oppressively in front of me. I hadn't really seen anything. I hadn't been looking to see. Something wrong with their clothes?

'I'll be up in a bit,' said Mrs Shaw.

There was a small amount of shuffling. Indirectly I watched. Mr Harbottle leant around her, familiar, composed, as he pushed the door shut on me with a bang.

It was a job of work getting up the stairs. I went the whole way in a violent frame of mind, upbraiding myself—you fool, you *fool*—though I didn't know for what. Suppose I had been my own grandfather, I thought, suppose I'd shown up by appointment to tune a piano, would this have been a ten-pound-note kind of a situation?

Mr Harbottle? Smug, portly Mr Harbottle, who wears two-tone shoes?

'I'll be up in a bit.' There had been a restrained softness in Mrs Shaw's voice.

You *fool*, I said to myself, have you learnt nothing in your life? It struck me that the words 'bewildered' and 'uncivilised' were related, or were they? Poor Bobbo, I thought, my teeth clenched, poor poor bloody Bobbo, with her Churches' Circle of Psychical Studies, and her stomach-turning *Blomchet*—I interrupted myself again—soaps—on the sudden thought that I'd be able to collect dust without climbing anything if I only swept it off the cistern above the loo. And yet I was seeing right before me that there were convenient little nests of the stuff in each corner I passed on the staircase. I had never spotted this before, but there they were.

By the time I'd let myself into my own flat, I was feeling angry with Mrs Shaw. Jesus, I said to myself, beneath my feet there's, what—carpet tiles, floorboards, joists, pipes and wires, builders' trash, I don't know, plasterboard, a lick of plaster, a splosh of off-colour paint, a few cubic litres of tainted air; but it's a world away downstairs.

Then, somewhat slow off the mark, I wondered: or is it?

I propped my crutches against the wall just inside the door and dumped my bag. I have a bike-messenger type bag which does very well if you're on crutches. Without the crutches, I got round into the kitchen and fetched out the dustpan and brush from under the sink. I don't dust much because I don't enjoy it, but I also don't because I can't manage it very well. I thought dusting a staircase might not be so bad, in that the surfaces to be swept, and my own feet, wouldn't perhaps need to be adjacent.

I went back out and down a flight and was bent facing a corner in the stairwell, sweeping, when a displaced creak in a board caused me to jerk upright and turn: I turned and then just stood there shocked to see Mr Harbottle dancing stealthily up towards me, portly Mr Harbottle—as I turned he hurtled up the last few steps, came upon me at speed swooping in towards my cheek, I felt polluted at his warm breath flooding the side of my face with words in the spew, warm and sweet, he had my good ear, he murmured, 'I've got my eye on you,' and was off again away down to the depths.

It was all over at once, but I remained frozen, in an attitude of surrender, like a bungled sylph from a side stall at an ice-carving show, I stood, frozen, and listened, contaminated, as he danced his way back down the stairs.

The phone started to ring in the flat. At my feet, on my feet, the dust had all spilled from the dust pan. Somehow, hobbledehoy, I answered the call in time.

'Ramble?'

'Yowch! Sorry, just catching my—yes?—wait a second.' I collapsed, in a controlled manner, onto the sofa.

'It's Anthony.'

Oh no, I thought, why, why did I answer this one?

'Where the hell is your husband?' he said.

I switched the handset. I keep thinking that if it's Con, I'll want a buffer of deafness when he speaks to me; but Anthony talks so quietly it borders on the offensive. I switched sides with the handset and bought myself a moment of disconnection.

Anthony's okay. He used to be Uncle Joe's copyist back in the days when film composers wrote scores by hand, and all the parts had to be copied by hand. The pair of them reminisce about it if you ask them, how Joe would be scoring right up to the wire on some hideous deadline with Anthony copying madly through the night and sometimes during half a day's recordings as well; rushing to the photocopy machine; copying parts for the afternoon's session while the morning's tracks were being laid. Nowadays, copyists extract and print parts direct from a score on computer. The beauty and clarity of the copyist's hand has become a recherché memory amongst the older sessions players.

Uncle Joe's life changed when he wrote a theme tune that became a hit. Work streamed in faster than he could manage, and Anthony started to orchestrate for him, until even with two of them at it they couldn't keep up. Anthony expanded duties again, to sidekick, manager, fixer and orchestrator. This was when the factory aspect got serious. They established a gang of satellite writers to help them out, of whom Con is the most recent and the youngest. He came on board as slop boy, powder monkey, jack of all work.

Con's desire to be an artist is supported as a vague ideal by his romantic mother, but not by his father, who is a bureaucrat, and who sticks to the standard of measurable graft. Con's father despises any activity that he deems 'coasting'. One of the few times I've been to visit them, I said, not that I meant it, 'How lucky you are. What a lovely garden.'

My father-in-law folded his arms across his chest, surveyed the prissy borders and replied, 'It's not luck.'

Despite this attitude, he declared later on that it was altogether sensible, it was an intelligent insurance policy, to cultivate a taste for wrecks and ruins. After all, *think about it*, that was how everything was going anyway.

This comment appeared to be a dig at his wife.

Con's orchestrating work is about the best his father could wish for, given that Con writes music at all. As for Con himself, to the extent that earning his living this way hampers his own output, and limits his time, he despairs over it.

I switched sides with the telephone. Where was my husband? 'Yes, Anthony, hello. Yes, he's out,' I said.

There was an extended silence before Anthony replied. 'Well basically, bugger that, you know? He called yesterday and left a message saying he wasn't well. So if he's well enough to go out, why isn't he here? I told him I want him to finish the job here. And what's the matter with him anyway? Has he been working? I've just this minute looked at the stuff he worked on on Friday and it's bars and bars of crap. Crap, if you want to know. We've got a flaming full orchestra booked for Thursday and Friday, and Con's Prague cues are unplayable, *and* what about the stuff he's supposed to have done since, quartet stuff? I mean last Friday's cues are literally unplayable and he had a day off yesterday, did he?—a day and a half now. You'd need the musicians on acid to even try and play it. Look,' Anthony had a coughing fit, 'look, what I'm saying is, he gets himself here sharpish, you got me? Because he's going to have to work straight bloody through, and I want him *here*. You know I don't like scheduling anyone to write more than two minutes a day, but dear Constantine's looking at pulling off more like five. The job's a bummer anyway, the whole job's a disaster waiting to happen, we shouldn't be doing it. I've got Bill in on it doing the pop cues, but it's the Prague scenes. We don't want to wing it there because that's where all the tender stuff happens in a bloody hotel in Prague. It's supposed to be lush and poignant and all that do-dah. We gave Con the Prague scenes because we thought he'd enjoy them. He's been a bit out of it, well okay, we all get the blues; but if he doesn't get himself in gear, I can't cover for him, and Joe will *never ever* use him again. I can give him as much coke as he wants, as he—' I was interested that Anthony hesitated over what he was saying; he retrenched, '—as he requires, what have you, because, believe me, he's not going to get much sleep. But he needs to be here and working by the end of the afternoon, this afternoon, *this* afternoon, you understand? I've got a full orchestra booked. There's no margin for having the bloody vapours. If he isn't here by about four o'clock, I'm blowing his gaff. I'll have to pull in someone else to redo this Prague botch-up and cover the rest myself, and that's not on. I don't care what's bothering him, you tell him he gets his bloody arse over here or it's finished. And by the way, he never pulls a stunt like this again, ever. He's good at what he does, but he's not *that* good.'

'Fair enough,' I said.

Occasionally people would say to my piano-tuner grand-father, in apprehensive tones, something like, 'Oh, God, yes, someone spilled wine on the keyboard a while ago. It was an accident. I wiped it up but I didn't know what else to do. So, yes, oh God, some of the notes have been sticking a bit: the octave below middle C. I'm sure you can fix it.'

In Grandfather's mind this was rather like saying, oh dear, you thought perhaps you'd just fed arsenic to your baby. Harshly, he'd reply, 'Fair enough.'

I put the phone down and found myself shaking with anger.

Con's not *that* good? And he phoned Anthony *yesterday*? And he's needed for all the *tender* stuff—in a *poignant* hotel, in *Prague*?

I rang his mobile but it wasn't switched on. If I had email at home, I could have emailed his mobile, but I don't.

'Fuck you,' I muttered, and then I said it again, louder.

'Expletive' dates to the late seventeenth century and originally meant any word deployed to plug a gap or buy time; but so commonplace was it amongst the English to string things out by swearing, that 'expletive' came loose from its moorings almost at once.

If you know how the word started out, a certain irony attaches to the phrase, found in censored transcripts, 'expletive deleted'. 'Expletive deleted' is no less an expletive, in the earliest sense of the term, than the unacceptable words it gets used to replace.

Well anyway, things have moved on. It would sound wrong to remark, for example, that poets in the past would occasionally mug it with an expletive when making up a shortfall in a metre—unless you were referring to Browning, who had the guts to use 'whew', and 'gr-r-r', and 'he-he', and 'forsooth'.

As I put the telephone back in its holder, a feeling of threat in my mind translated into the idea that if I could only fix my meter, Mr Harbottle would leave me alone. Leaving me alone, in this fantastical equation, felt as though it had necessarily to entail his leaving Mrs Shaw alone also—which was, of course, nonsense, not to mention the fact that, just because I got the meter done, it wouldn't solve the problem of the rent. But other than photocopy a tenner over and over again, I find the matter of the rent remains unaddressable by me.

At least I could do the meter.

Nothing was going to make me sweep the stairs a second time. Instead, I went up to the bathroom and swept off the top of the loo cistern, and also, once I realised it would do, the medicine cabinet. Both surfaces are just above head height. The excess dust that wafted down made me blink, but I didn't have to climb anything.

When I set to work in the meter cupboard, with a candle burning on the floor, the usual kind of trash in my head had me thinking that the command, 'dust this cake', would normally be taken to mean that a layer of icing sugar or cocoa powder had to be shaken over cake X. However, I thought, if the order happened to be being made on behalf of Miss Havisham, it would imply that dust already on the cake wanted removing. Like 'secrete', or 'cleave', I thought, 'dust' was an example of a word with opposite meanings attached.

Cleave, secrete; Mr Harbottle and Mrs Shaw; none of my business: *dust*.

In the drawer with the artificial waterflower wondershells, the Mecanorma Graphoplex, the envelope with the photograph of the Nazi man and boy outside the Jewish hat shop, and so on, I found another envelope, brown, that Stella Ramble had hoarded. It contained three different types of paper: a clipped out, ancient piece of newsprint with an article on it entitled 'The Law as to Flirting', another photograph, and the order of service for a funeral.

The photograph showed Alphonso Ramble, with, at his side—both of them in dinner jackets—his friend the clock fanatic—the clock fanatic a very Burt Lancaster to Alphonso's Fred Astaire. I call this man the clock fanatic because he rang my grandmother every evening at nine and spoke to her for exactly five minutes. While they spoke, she would laugh a girlish laugh that I never otherwise heard. No one else answered the phone in my grandparents' house when it went at nine o'clock.

For what it's worth, 'The Law as to Flirting' reads as follows:

When does society take cognisance of the fact that a married woman is accepting attentions from men other than her husband, so as to indicate in some positive, social way, disapprobation of such proceedings? The rule of society is that society has no business to recognise anything of the kind until the husband does. For as long as a husband expresses no disapprobation of what his wife is doing, her conduct is to be regarded as something with which nobody else has any concern. This is, however, a rule so liberal that society adheres to it in only a modified form. The kindness of a husband has not always protected his wife in a social way.

Inside the order of service for the clock fanatic's funeral, which took place, by chance, only a few months after Alphonso's, was folded a photocopy of the vicar's address:

We give thanks to the Lord for the life of someone who has truly been described as a gentleman. His family have told me some of their special memories; his love of fuchsias and hatred of slugs! His cold swim every morning at seven o'clock.

120

Everyone here will probably have their own memories of his insistence on punctuality, and I myself remember well being reprimanded quite severely when I arrived for supper one evening at a few minutes past eight! He was never a minute out of time himself, and the family have told me that he always telephoned his beloved wife from the office every day at twelve o'clock sharp.

Right there I stopped taking in the words on the page, though my eyes continued to skim across the platitudes that followed.

I can't vouch for this, this may be another fact that isn't true, but I vaguely remember that, if you go back far enough, there are maps of London that have St Paul's in the middle surrounded by concentric circles, each successive circle representing a second's lag in the time it would take for the sound of the bells to travel. As I recall it, these maps allowed fanatics to set their clocks accurately to the bells of St Paul's, no matter that they lived some way away.

Elsewhere in the land, I think people didn't much care. When England was first connected up by telegraph, it came to public attention that the time in different places was out of sync. This led to many jokes. It would have been a faux pas, in 1849, for a polite maiden to betray to her suitor knowledge of his intent to ask for her hand. Most unfortunate, therefore, if through telegraphic communication,

a young lady might appear to have affirmatively answered in Devonshire an important question—say, seven minutes and a half before, according to local clocks, it had actually been proposed to her in London.

Whew!

The clock fanatic called his two ladies at noon and at nine. Did time for the three of them feel the same? I suspect the clock fanatic acted like the accurate bell, and that his ladies conceived of themselves as dwelling on different but concentric circles of his attention.

When I was emptying out her house, I asked Stella Ramble what had happened to her tailor's dummy. She laughed delightedly, and still knew the answer.

'Well, Graham Loring'—I had never heard of Graham Loring—'is such a frightful old roué. He always said I had the smartest figure of anyone he knew. He asked me recently if he could have the dummy because, you know, it was modelled on me. What a dreadful bore that was. He asked me for it, so I let him take it away. His wife is *such a dear*, of course.'

The clock fanatic's wife I met several times, a quiet, thin lady confined to an expensive wheelchair. I don't know whether or not she too was 'such a dear', but let's give her the benefit of the doubt: I bet she was.

Only when I'd finished executing Mrs Shaw's instructions re the meter did it strike me that I could have got a thousand times as much dust as I needed by puncturing the hoover bag.

The air in the cupboard was dense not only with dust and hairspray fumes, but with smoke from the guttering candle. I felt woozy. I dumped the can on one of the book shelves in the main room, not for any reason beyond thinking that, as it would be out of place there, I'd be bound to keep noticing it and would remember to give it back.

After tidying up, I went and had a bath. I was dirty, tired

and miserable, and the slight float one experiences in a bath feels good with aching ligaments or whatever. My mother has large breasts which, when she lies in a bath, rise up above the surface and get cold; but I don't have this problem.

When I was little, I used to sit on the loo seat and yatter at my mother while she lounged about in the bath after breakfast on Sunday mornings. She didn't make a point of answering, but she didn't send me away either.

I lay, submerged, and found myself returning to Mrs Shaw, in particular to this question: how much of the information she'd given me about my business had I, myself, provided to her first? Con must have said something or other, clearly he had, but did it need to have been all that much? Our marriage has foundered. I don't notice things. What else?

I then considered the following. How did I know that she'd done anything more to the meter than wipe some of the dust off with the side of her hand? Maybe the whole exercise had been a game on her part. But if so, to what end?

I didn't know what I was thinking, except it then crossed my mind that Mrs Shaw, this morning, spent time in the flat alone when I asked her to fetch my brace. Suppose she lifted something while she was at it? In Victorian slang, that would make her, not a burglar, but a 'sneak thief', i.e. one who doesn't break to enter. Goldilocks, for example, is a sneak thief with regard to the little bear's porridge, if a vandal as regards its furniture.

I got annoyed with the way my mind was going, told myself that my doubts about Mrs Shaw were flim flam, and that it was pointless to worry about her being a thief even if she was one, as the only items I could think of that I would mind her stealing were certain books, and I doubted that she had the know-how of a competent book thief. I wasn't going to get out of the bath straight away simply in order to check. I said to myself: if she has, improbably, stolen your favourite books, it will be possible over time to replace them.

When Alphonso died, Stella Ramble threatened to get rid of his entire library, so my father took it. When my father died, my stepmother threatened ditto, so I ditto. My stepmother has never forgiven any of us for the fact that my father's life ended in my mother's house—after he'd been talking to my mother—on what was once our family staircase.

It's an odd outcome, amid these seasick relationships, that I have been forced to house most of Alphonso's books, still in boxes, in my bedroom at my mother's. She tried to repossess this room when I got married. She had a desire to make her dwelling place perfect. I said, 'Make the rest of it as perfect as you like, but leave one room for me, please. You can't tell me you need the space. You've never needed it before. Please, please, please. What are you going to do, put a fancy man in there? You have a whole, proper house. What am I supposed to do? Please don't get rid of my things. Think of it as me doing you a favour: it'll give you something new to grumble about with your friends.'

She replied, 'I have more than enough to grumble about with my friends.'

Luckily she caved in, and I still have box upon box in my old bedroom at home. I selected out what looked to me like the most interesting books, and took away as many as we had space for in the flat. Once I started to read these volumes, I found I liked my forebears very much. One of them had thumbed the pages soft and dirty on Alfred Crowquill's *Electric Telegraph of*

Fun, 1854. This excellent little work contains hundreds of jokes of the following variety: 'A clergyman was censuring a young lady for tight lacing. "Why," replied Miss, "you would not surely recommend *loose habits* to your parishioners!"'

Better yet is Ally Sloper, the pre-eminent comic character of a now-forgotten, late nineteenth-century English consciousness. Ally Sloper singlehandedly links—across all the decades that separate them—Mr Micawber to Charlie Chaplin. It would have been 100 per cent fitting for Mrs Shaw to have filched my 1884 copy of an *Ally Sloper's Magazine*. Why was Mr Alexander Sloper, con man and drunkard, named for his trick of sloping off down alleys away from Poppin's Court? The answer is that he always made himself scarce when the rent collector called. A typical Sloperian joke goes like this: 'When is a settled account like water to A. Sloper?—When it is liquid-hated.'

Nowadays, we think of such humour as being suited to an ice lolly stick, an 80p comic or a Christmas cracker; as being suited, that is, to a child. Why? Because all the English collude in civilising their children with bad jokes.

Better even than Crowquill or Ally Sloper is *Hood's Own*, which I have inherited in an early two-volume edition. The second vol. has a receipt tucked between two pages showing that one of my Irish ancestors had this, I take it, deeply loved work rebound in Morocco, at a cost of three shillings and sixpence, on January the 4th, 1896. The printed section of the receipt reads: '..............189 M.............. Bought of C. Coxhead, 4 Southwood Lane, Highgate, Hosier, Haberdasher, Stationer. Berlin & Fleecy Wools, Scotch Yarns, &c. Monthly Magazines and Bookbinding. Agents for Eastman's Chemical Dye Works.'

I love *Hood's Own*. It has more bad jokes in it than any other work I possess. The one I like best is this:

ABSTRACTION

After noticing that the caption is a pun, you think, well, only half a pun perhaps, as what's illustrated is essentially two different forms of theft; but that's fine, because, if only half a pun, then the sum is half pun, half engaging idea, which is fine. Or perhaps it's two fifths bad pun, one fifth engaging idea and two fifths *nice pictures*. From Mrs Shaw's perspective, the paired vols. stolen together might fetch, say, a hundred and fifty quid.

A work I find troubling by comparison is Stella Ramble's Berlin book, *Berlin*, 1928, introductory text by Alfred Döblin, with photographs by the Austro-Croatian baron, Mario von Bucovich. In mint condition this would fetch more than the Hood; but my copy is coverless and stained, and anyway, its value to me is outside any system I care to quantify.

You might think that, to Stella Ramble, its worth would lie principally in the handwritten: '*Zur Erinnerung an Berlin! von Papa*'. Had the book helped her remember Berlin? Had it helped her remember *Papa*? After Beata translated the inscription for me, I made a special trip to the old people's home to ask. I had already shown Stella Ramble the photograph of the hat shop. When I took in the Berlin book, she was in sharper focus; though once again, the phantom 'Fuesenberg' concentration camp got a mention.

For all the time I've known her, Stella Ramble has, in the old phrase, been 'living on unkindly terms with her years'. I've understood this since I was tiny and found myself staring at the cream pots on her dressing table.

Now I am living on unkindly terms with her years as well. Above all, I find it distressing that she no longer remembers her own stories. They started to disintegrate before I recognised what was happening, and soon, when I questioned her over curious details that I myself only cloudily remembered, she had little grasp of what I was talking about. As an example, I became convinced for a while that an anecdote she had once told me, about having surgery as a young girl, could not in every particular be true.

She had said, roughly speaking, 'I had my beastly appendix out at home when I was little, lying on the ironing board. And for a month after that, if I went anywhere in the house, I had to be carried by the butler.'

Surely, not the craziest surgeon, not *Frankenstein*, would use an ironing board for an operating table?

Con and I don't have an ironing board. One day I was ironing a shirt for him on top of our two blankets, the pink and the yellow, which I'd spread out across the bedroom table, otherwise known as my desk—where I'm sitting right now—when it came to me that if you were a surgeon in the early part of the twentieth century performing a messy operation on someone at home—and only the poor were forced to risk going to hospital—then a table in the servants' quarters, laid over with blankets, would probably have seemed ideal.

When were ironing boards invented? I don't know. I couldn't check with Stella Ramble because she wouldn't have had the faintest clue what I was on about. Ironing boards? An appendix? Frankenstein?

She did, however, when I first asked her, have enough long-term memory intact to tell me something about Berlin.

When I moved her into the old people's home, she went very mad for a spell. I discovered in short order that 'EMI' meant Elderly Mentally Infirm, i.e. dotty, and that 'DNR' meant Do Not Resuscitate, i.e., yes, on my authority, let her die.

She settled, got her new bearings and sobered up, but this brief revival was the last time I was able to get even semi-cogent answers out of her. Since then she has declined dramatically, losing more and more of herself, of everybody, of everything she's ever known.

'I did go to Berlin, yes,' she said, 'when I was quite young.'

'You never mentioned this before.'

'Oh well.'

'If it's any help, I don't know when you arrived there, but you left again on about the 26th of June, 1929.'

'Darling, you are wonderfully clever. Don't be *too* clever.'

'Why were you there? What were you doing?'

'Pff,' she said genially, 'Aunty Gol knew a chap, knew a chap. He was head of a big company. He lived on a very swish road off the Brandenburg Gate.'

'Which road?'

'North East?'

'Okay.'

'He wanted an English girl to live-in. It was very frightening there, nobody spoke a word of English. He was very, very rich. Every morning I went with him in his Maybach car, marvellous car. We went to the Tiergarten, "the Hyde Park of Berlin". We'd get out with a dictionary, and walk across, and the chauffeur would meet us on the other side. The chauffeur spoke a little English, he was very helpful when I got into difficulties. I was fond of him. Papa had three teenage children and a horrid little boy of about seven. I had to spend my days with the horrid little boy. We went out every weekend in the frightfully swanky car. Every evening I went to fetch Papa in the car. I always called him Papa. He had an ageing mother, she was rather disagreeable and tiresome. And she was enormous, very heavy. When she got in the car it sank with a great wallop. They did have a certain style of social life, but they had a very stuffy family life. It wasn't fun, Lord! But the children were fed like grown-ups, I mean they never produced special boring food for the children. They were Jewish. I was very shocked because they put the dirty sheets out of their rooms in heaps on the landings even when they had blood on them, nobody cared. I did it for over a year. By the end I was rather thankful to go home. The worst was that Papa's wife had nervous attacks. She had to go and stay outside Berlin.'

'Where?'

'North. You went on the train. Was it *Fuesenberg*? When she went she always went with a dear friend. She didn't like going alone. But one time the friend was ill and I was asked to go. Really it was a loony bin with a terrific forest where you went for walks. She always had to have a gun, she had it in her handbag. She would take frights sometimes. She was scared witless of what she called "bad men"—woodcutters—it was quite terrifying sometimes. She would take to her heels like a hare and I knew I'd get lost if I didn't keep up with her. The asylum was frightfully expensive; frightfully good food. Afterwards they turned it into a concentration camp.'

'What happened to them in the war?' I asked.

'Oh, one didn't go into that sort of thing.'

'You never found out what happened to *Papa* in the war? His family?'

'One didn't go into that sort of thing.'

'Really?'

'Not really, no.'

I was conscious, as I had this conversation, that I was talking to a woman who, in her thirties, had had the terminal joints of her little toes removed so she could wear more elegant shoes.

I got myself—as ever, with care—out of the bath. I was upstairs anyway so I thought I might have a pop at the ice piece. I told myself sternly that I was going to do it this time: time was running out. But once I was sitting ready, all primed to write, I couldn't bear to work on shlock.

~

I had planned but failed to go to the Minimart on the way home from the library. When it came to be supper time I realised I hadn't yet had lunch. I went down—no books missing—and looked in the kitchen cupboard where I found spaghetti and rice, neither of which I could face, and a box of packet soups which I thought I could, though when I sat in front of a mugful, the same green colour as pond scum—what is the scientific name for pond scum?—I could drink no more than a mouthful or two. I tipped the rest down the sink, made a coffee, with unfrothed milk, sat down in front of that instead and burst into tears.

I cried, though for what or for whom I didn't really know.

I don't hate music. It was careless of Con to say so. I've found music hard to take since my father fell down the stairs.

After some time what I was crying about was my work. It's hardly my worst problem, doesn't rate at all really, I just have to do it; but perhaps it was the most sensible problem to cry about for that very reason. I have only two full days left to write the ice piece. I said to myself, the less time I give it, the more gratifyingly efficient I will end up having been; except that, viewed as a whole, my life is so far from any rational sense of efficiency, I hardly knew what I thought I meant by this.

A small part of my mind suggested that perhaps I'd simply fail to finish the job, would fail to meet my deadline for the first time ever; but given the penalties, I didn't really believe this.

Shortly after ten o'clock, I heard Mr and Mrs Shaw yelling. I checked the clock on the oven: it was five past. I'd slipped into dreaming in an airy sort of way, but the two of them brought me up cold. I was stiff and sore from sitting for so long on one of the hard kitchen chairs.

Their fight lasted a few minutes and then as far as I could hear it stopped completely. It was painful getting to my feet. I made my way up to the bathroom to clean my teeth.

*

This morning, when I came up to the flat from downstairs and found that Mrs Shaw had put the pillow and pink blanket not on the bed but on the sofa, I left them there thinking I might spend tonight on the sofa. But now that it comes to it, I guess I'll sleep in bed after all, in case—in case she—Mrs Shaw, I'm thinking, so—so, once again the solitary bed.

~

I lay down and found myself turning over in my mind how, on a night bus, during the hours of real darkness, you some- times catch a glimpse inside a hunting creature's eye, or you perhaps make out a handful of stars, but much of the time all you see through the window is lurid, manufactured flashes.

Even where these flashes are interpretable as people's windows, or petrol stations, or rest-stop signage, it's an effort to attach to them any idea of humanity, notwithstanding the fact that, superimposed across every dislocated fragment of this view, you have a dim reflection of your own face.

I thought to myself about how, when you're on a night bus and the driver drives into a wall of rain, the distortions can become so great that you quietly cease to feel like a being from the real world of newspapers and photocopy machines.

I lay and I thought. I was dead beat, but for a long time, some hours, I didn't sleep, just lay, just thinking, and listened, despite myself. And I heard nothing. Nothing. All I heard in all that time was patient, unwitnessing silence.

5

Wednesday

This morning I woke, dragged over to Con's side of the bed, flicked off the alarm clock switch, tried to calm myself, then got up. I decided to make a coffee and start at once on my work, but as I trudged slowly down to the kitchen, there was Mrs Shaw banging at the flat door. Annoyance hit me first, then the same diffuse mortification I'd felt knocking on hers.

She was wearing yet another pair of heels, boots this time, patent.

'Oh dear, I'm so sorry.' My stomach tightened. 'You didn't really need to come up.'

'I said didn't I?'

'You did. Thank you. And I have your hairspray. But I've done the meter now. I managed it after all. I'm so sorry I bothered you.'

I thought about Mr Harbottle leaning around her downstairs, and wanted to ask whether she was okay.

'Let's have a see.' She bent into the cupboard. 'Don't half stink in here.' She was amused. She pulled back out. 'How d'you do that then?'

'Is it all right? I just did what you said.'

'Course it is. You could get work cleaning up like that.'

'Cleaning up?'

She gave me a look. 'You clean it for real, they'll be onto you even if you ain't done nothing wrong. Who cleans their meters? No one. You done the dust natural like it should be. You done all right.'

It didn't strike me as much of an accomplishment but I was childishly pleased.

'Mr Harbottle didn't look,' I said, 'at least, not while I was here. I don't know what he wanted.'

Mrs Shaw replied in a voice so deadly that I felt myself stiffen the way a cat does when you grip it round the back of the neck. 'Mr *Harbottle* wants his *rent*.'

My mouth flooded with a bitter taste. I thought again about my piano-tuner grandfather having ten-pound notes pressed into his hand.

When he told me about this transaction, I, being young, and indoctrinated with his high notion of piano tuners, asked him, was it proper in such circumstances to take the cash?

He explained to me that it would have been yet more humiliating for the men in question had he refused.

I was fascinated by this, the idea that he had taken their money as an act of charity almost—that it had been graceful on his part to collude in the pretence that it was they who were humiliating him.

As I stood with Mrs Shaw, I lacked all grace. All I could think to say was, 'Coffee?'

'Don't mind if I do,' she said. 'I could look at a biscuit as well.'

I wasn't sure about biscuits, but luckily there was about enough coffee left for me to make some for us both. Because I botched the way I managed the spoon, the mound of milk froth in Mrs Shaw's cup this time had a nipple-like stain in the middle. She laughed.

When I sat down opposite her at the kitchen table, I found myself saying, 'If I were to ask you what's the best story you—' she cut me short with a wave, '—you know, if—' I took her to mean that she did have a best story. Many people, most perhaps, don't.

She was looking slick, in a white, synthetic waistcoat, styled, like a war reporter's, with numerous pockets, and pockets within pockets, out of one of which she pulled a lighter and a packet of cigarettes. She opened them up, and as she smoked, flicked the ash into the lid.

The fridge was making a grumblesome noise, which loomed with the tobacco in the air we were breathing.

Mrs Shaw's ash pile grew but she said nothing, until our silence became uncompanionable I felt. Perhaps the wave with which she had cut me short had meant, 'forget it'. I tried to distract myself by thinking, *he's left you*, you weren't good enough, *he's gone*, he's disappeared, *he's gone*, &c.—but this wasn't a help. I finished my coffee, down to the slowly sliding last remains of milk froth, gave up on Mrs Shaw, and became restive; but simultaneous with my saying, 'I forgot the biscuits,' she stubbed out her cigarette and said, 'So in Spain, right—'

I had already semi risen. I went and rummaged in the cupboard, where I found a tin of shortbread on the top shelf I could reach, how old I wasn't sure. I didn't recognise it. It looked like a Christmas present type item. I was telling myself that Mrs Shaw's false start—'So in Spain, right'—was no doubt not the first four words of the best story she knew, but merely the start of the only one she could remember.

I had already finished my coffee. I needed to get to work on the ice piece. It was something like fifty hours to my deadline. Beyond the deadline a prisoner can be shot. I dumped the shortbread in front of her with the tin still Sellotaped shut.

'You want to hear?' she said.

I sat back down again feeling both irritated and a little ashamed.

'So in Spain, right,' she began to pick at the Sellotape with her clickety, pearlescent fingernails, 'couple of summers back, I get this off of a woman what knows the girl. Her view: they was muck because their cousins had ate this donkey what was deceased of just being old.'

The idea of ostracising people for eating animals that have died of natural causes, falls way outside my normal frame of reference. I manoeuvred myself on my chair seat ready to listen properly, sat sideways, in the end, with my back against the wall.

'I know what you're thinking,' said Mrs Shaw.

She didn't know what I was thinking.

'So anyway, right, there's this seaside town, right, and there's this girl. No—I mean, right, there's this bloke, right, it's like the Mafia: small town, right, there's this bloke like the Mafia what has the police, well, he's got everyone—they can't touch him. He's called The Gun. They can't touch him, police, nobody. He's got his people and he's got this town nailed. So this girl's going home from work one evening, he grabs her and he pulls her down into the basement of this house and he rapes her. It's bad, right, and she's fighting him to the nail—'

'Tooth and nail,' I said—for some stupid reason I'd never thought of Spanish houses as having basements.

'You what?' Mrs Shaw finally got the shortbread tin open.

'Sorry, I take it back. Sorry.' *I take it back*? What was the matter with me? I could feel her looking me over and was relieved when she decided to continue.

'So she sticks up for herself, but it's bad,' Mrs Shaw picked out a triangle of shortbread then simply held it, 'and he does her good and proper—like, really bad, like. So when she makes it back home, she makes it back home, and her dad, he's like this decent geezer, right: gutted, can't even speak. Walks out, goes straight round the police and he walks in and there's this young kid on the desk filling in a form or whatever, other officers are all in the back, and the dad, he says, like, "I've come to report a crime." And the kid looks up and he's, "Yes?" And the dad says, "The Gun just raped my daughter." Kid looks back down at his piece of paper and he says, "What are you talking about, old man? I ain't heard of no Gun. Clear off out of it and go back home to bed." So the dad, he walks out, goes home, gets this knife, and he starts prowling around. Seaside town, right, little streets, alleys? So, small hours, he's been out there half the night, he sees The Gun on his tod down this poky little passageway, no one anywhere, right, so he goes down and he knifes him and he kills him. Then he goes back round the police, right: same kid on the desk. So like, the dad, like, he says, "I've come to report a crime." Kid looks up, like, "Yes?" Dad's like, "I've just murdered The Gun." Kid looks down again. He don't say nothing. He says, "Who's this Gun then? Never heard of him. Take yourself back home, old man, and put yourself to bed."'

I looked at Mrs Shaw. She grinned at me and I grinned back.

I liked the story hugely. The more I thought about it, the more I liked it. Not only was its shape faultless, but it ended with a perfect lie. How wonderful, I thought, she's told me a story that ends with a perfect lie.

Mrs Shaw began to eat her piece of shortbread, shoving the tin towards me with her right-hand fourth fingernail, but I didn't want any.

'You don't eat hardly nothing.'

'I'm not so hungry.' I shrugged. 'Things are a bit cockeyed just now, in my life I mean. Well—you know that.'

'Don't you take nothing or nothing?' She made an explanatory gesture in the direction of her lap.

'What, for this?' I asked, gesturing at my own. 'The brace is pretty good. I've been wearing it more, recently. I ought to wear it all the time really.' *Why, replied Miss, you would not surely recommend* loose habits *to your parishioners!*

'And I do have painkillers,' I said, 'but I try to avoid them. I have a high pain threshold whatever that means. That's what the doctors say to me. It seems a funny thing to say. What are you tolerating if it doesn't hurt yet? I don't know. Pain is kind of interesting but it's also tedious. It's not that I like it or anything, but it's good for telling you how much damage you're doing. It tells you when to stop ahead of the point where you can't carry on any more anyway. It's like the red section on a petrol gauge. If I take painkillers, I so-to-speak disable my petrol gauge; but I'm not some gruelling purist. I do take stuff now and again. After a certain point there's no point in *not* taking anything. I have DF118 pills for when I'm at my worst: like codeine sort of thing. Also other stuff, but not as strong.'

Goodness, I thought, that was a long speech!

'You should dose up more.'

'You sound like my husband,' I said. 'The thing is, I patch together again fast, usually, it's not so bad. If I've gone too far it's only a couple of days or something to be back to functional normal, usually, two or three days. It doesn't specially matter. Other people have infinitely worse problems than me.'

'Don't give me that,' she said. 'I don't think you know what you're doing to yourself.'

I shrugged again.

'You heard from him or what?'

'No.'

'You ain't tried to find him?'

'No.'

'You don't want him back then?'

'You don't know where he is do you?' My question was as near as we came to acknowledging that Mr Shaw had returned.

'I don't. I don't know nothing about it. If I find something out, I find something out, but I don't ask.'

'Well, I haven't found anything out,' I said.

'What you going to do then? You talked to anyone? Your mum?'

'Absolutely not, she's the last—actually, I did think about calling one of my friends yesterday, briefly, but, it's hard to explain, she's too straight. And what is there to say, really? I don't know.'

Other people have girlfriends they confide in. I have Beata. When we've ever talked on intimate subjects, it has always felt to me as though we were breaking some sort of an agreement; and yet, just as she is, she's a fact of my life for which I'm grateful.

'Straight's all right,' said Mrs Shaw.

'Of course. I don't mean anything against her. I'll tell you something though. When she's talking she says, "memo to self". I've never told anyone this, but I hate the way she says, "memo to self". *Hey, how are you?*—memo to self: I must buy a packet of paper—*how's things, what's up?* It's silly of me, I know, and anyway, that's nothing to do with it. She just wouldn't be the right person.'

'You saying, you tell her, she'll go for him herself?'

'No,' I said, 'no, no, hardly. No, she doesn't like him, never has. Absolutely not. I can't explain but that's way off beam.'

'You think you know but you don't.'

'Well I do think I know,' I said, and we left it at that.

I rather imagined Mrs Shaw might go back downstairs at this point, but she didn't. She said, 'Was you close to your dad then?'

Johnson is phoning me tomorrow, I thought out of nowhere.

I pictured myself getting up and washing the coffee cups, or the frother. I imagined myself saying that I needed to clean the floor. I happened to be staring with attention at the dirty, chequerboard floor. It would have required her to go somewhere else if I'd started to clean the floor because her feet were on the floor. I was thinking these thoughts, about the floor and so on, as I heard myself say, 'Oh yes. Apart from anything else'—I snapped into sharp focus—'you know, besides being my father, he was also my third cousin once removed.'

'Come again?'

'It doesn't matter. I mean it's true. I mean, yes, we were close.'

'You was cousins with your dad?' Mrs Shaw sounded incredulous.

'I am therefore also cousins with myself, as it happens. It

140

isn't so unusual. Hey, we didn't eat dead pigeons out of the gutter, okay.'

She laughed. She was amused again. When she's amused it's catching, so I felt quite amused myself for a few seconds. Then she said, 'So what was you on about about your legs—arthritis or something?'

I had no idea why we were having this conversation. Had I started it? I didn't know why she was asking me these things, and I especially didn't know why I was answering her. '*Septic arthritis*,' I said in a bright voice. 'I got an infection in my hip right after I left school: left school, left home. All the time I was at school I was completely healthy, never broke a bone, never had my tonsils out, nothing, just flu or, you know. Then I left and almost immediately, !*bam*!, fever—why? No one could say. Pain: catastrophic, *rapid destruction of the joint*, a few weeks in hospital, out again, gee, fairly rare condition. Tough beans; sorry, but you're going to walk—' I rocked my hands like a see-saw, 'from here on out. Not as bad as it could be, though; and, hey, when you've walked badly for, oh, thirty years or so, at a guess, looking at you?—we'll give you a new hip, in about thirty years, when you've ground the joint down that much further. Okay, fine, thanks very much: this I can deal with, aches a bit, never mind. But then a couple of years ago I got stuck with pelvic dysfunction as well. Joke over, because the limp from the hip happens to be the very thing to—it—it inflicts stress on the pelvic ligament. The first condition is, in effect, exactly calculated to make the second one worse; one of those cases where irony lacks for a humorous edge.'

Mrs Shaw sighed a sigh that implied, I think: fuck-off-to-gobbledygook.

'The pelvic thing—' why, *why* was I continuing?—'is pregnancy related, although I lost it. I mean I—I lost it. I mean what I mean is, I got worse even after I lost it, oddly. I was described as an exceptional case, which, in this particular instance, it's not a good thing to be. You know how it goes.'

I hadn't been aware that I was watching Mrs Shaw, but I here registered that she'd become preternaturally motionless. My mind flooded with such noise that I was in difficulties for how to continue. I worried that I hadn't explained properly even though I didn't want to be explaining at all. 'It was a stillbirth. They came here in an ambulance. When a baby dies in the womb, it was, they—but, inside my head, inside myself, you know what? I don't care. He's completely real to me.'

Mrs Shaw fell so far into thought that I found myself able to examine her.

She has laughter lines even in repose.

'You're all right,' she said after a while. 'He's real to me too.'

I don't know what we talked about next, but I noticed she was wearing a diamond ring. I can't tell a natural diamond from a fake one, so perhaps it wasn't diamond but zircon, if that's the right word. *Zircona*? I didn't think she'd been wearing it before. Was it a gesture of apology from Mr Shaw, or a bribe, or perhaps her cut in a division of spoils?

Somewhere along the line I asked her to fill me in on meter fraud. It came up, I don't remember how. She gave me an unwilling and far from clear account of the whole thing viewed as a business. I didn't fully understand her, not least because of all the slang terms she used—I tried and failed to memorise them as she spoke—but I gather there's a hundred different ways to fiddle a meter.

In larger places, clubs and the like, or commercial greenhouses, including illicit ones presumably—I'm saying illicit: she didn't mention it—but in a place of this kind, with a consistent, heavy drain on power, in back-street factories for all I know, it's common either to plumb a separate meter in and out, or to use a black box whatever that is—well, an electrical device the size of a tub of ice cream, she described it with her hands—to pull off some of the numbers.

Domestically, meanwhile, just in their houses, people have innumerable tricks, from using magnets to slow things down, to tinkering with a screwdriver to cause the meter to run backwards: whatever.

The crucial element in all this, once you're up and doing it, is to regulate for how long. This much I did understand. A normal person at home causing a utility meter to run backwards does so one month in three. One month backwards, one month forwards: roughly zero on the dial. The third month you rack up numbers for your bill. If your usage is consistent for its quarter, and for unseasonable weather patterns if that applies, then no questions asked. Alternatively, if you have a system that bypasses your ordinary meter, you leave the device in place for as long as will give you a balance that looks adequately plausible.

What Mrs Shaw's husband is involved in in Bedford is a service that takes care of these switches back and forth, on various systems; that rents out and installs the black boxes and spare meters; that circulates them between clients so they are in use as much as possible, bearing in mind the varying schedules of the utility company meter-readers, who, however, in the way of such things, are sometimes being bought off; that keeps tabs on every aspect of the game—all in all a mathematical headache requiring the very skills, I'd have thought, that are looked for in an unambitious bank manager.

I didn't ask Mrs Shaw why she and her husband had been forced to leave town, perhaps it had been credit cards; but it wasn't hard to see that with the meter business there could be screw-ups, kickings—feral-pigeon type turf wars.

'I've never heard of any of this,' I said.

'I just told you.'

'Well, yes.'

'So now you have,' she said. 'You now,' she added, 'you had yours backwards two weeks I'm presuming, gives you sort of like a third off of your normal bill. That looks wrong that does, that's why I was pissy about it when I come up.'

'*Two* weeks? You've only been here one week, haven't you, roughly speaking?'

'You don't notice nothing,' she said. 'Right, two weeks yesterday we been here.' She stopped and chose another piece of shortbread, square, though they must all taste the same. 'Why you think what you do,' she said, 'first week we was leery, but then it was, *fuck that*, and we started fighting.'

The mention of the two of them fighting caused me to glance reflexively at the clock on the oven.

'I must be completely mad,' I said. 'I have to write a piece for Friday and I'm nowhere with it. I have to get cracking.' I waved towards the magazines on the counter.

'I'll push off then.'

Though she stood up, I had the feeling she wanted to talk

some more. She fiddled with her cigarette packet, emptying the lid into the rubbish.

It was only when I heard the flat door close behind her that I found myself wondering, for the very first time, what it is that she herself does.

Mrs Shaw went, and I got as far as the main room—all six-steps' worth—when I thought on a whim to give myself the Roberts Dynatron experience, which is to say that I picked out a CD, selected a track and put the volume to full.

I hovered on Con's piano stool, immersed for five minutes in a spare and lucid version of the jazz standard, *Walkin'*—cool as a breeze. I tormented myself, that is. What possessed me? Only a cripple would sit still for this.

Music cues written for the movies divide into two basic kinds: those that play with a scene and those that play against. I don't mean there aren't further subtleties involved, but when the score is first hashed out, this is the primary distinction to be drawn. To play with, you put schmaltzy music under a schmaltzy scene. To play against, you might put, under that same schmaltzy scene, oh, music to suggest that the merry heroine will soon be being eviscerated by her landlord.

Even if a movie audience weren't to recognise the name of the tune, to lay any version of *Walkin'* under a scene featuring a cripple would have to constitute playing against—unless this happened to be a very special kind of cripple who somehow actually was as cool as a breeze.

Once in a while I'll put on a track or two with the volume appallingly loud just to make my ears believe they can hear. That's what this was: five minutes of conversation between the music and my ears. But I rarely play music now, and only when I'm by myself. At home—I mean at my mother's house—I never played any. It was my parents who made the noise. My father taught me the piano until he left, but then he left. Of course he took his piano with him. Of course my mother didn't get another one. After the removals men had gone she said, 'At last, a bit of space.'

To my surprise, she made no adjustments in her listening habits. She'd got so used to being loud, she didn't think to jig the Dynatron's volume button downwards; unless she was blocking out the silence instead, but I don't think so.

As I sat and listened to the music, it came to me—I was taken aback—that I felt loose and not-unhappy. Then I suddenly understood that, as well as all the rest of it, these past few days I've been waiting for something.

The moment passed. I went back upstairs to my desk where Mrs Shaw's questions once again pressed in on me. I couldn't so easily throw off the mood they had invoked. Not for the first time, I felt punished remembering how, when I'd found out I was pregnant, my greatest fear had been that I wouldn't love the baby enough, not that it would die.

The word 'ambulance' originally meant a walking hospital, but no one could have reached me in time, whatever ambulance means. An 'ambulance' was a hospital that was walked behind a war.

When I was eight or nine, I accompanied my mother to tea with a woman she visited only rarely. We had to drive for ages to get to her house, which was tall with long windows. We were guided to an upstairs drawing room.

The sun burned. The curtains, dropping to the floor, were only part way open, so that the light slanted in dazzlingly, leaving the rest of the room in deep shadow. A great vase with whole branches of lilac in it, in the gloom in a corner, gave out a sweetness so potent that it quenched every other perfume including my mother's eau de toilette, which she had spurted onto her throat just before getting out of the car.

My mother's friend spoke of a sister who had had one child but had never fallen in love with it. 'She denies this—would do myself!—but doesn't know the difference, not a clue, doesn't know what it's *like* to fall in love with your baby, doesn't see what's missing. I hardly have to say that I *do* see it. Fell in love with both of mine, know the difference.'

My mother had just then taken a bite of cake. She nodded. Given the risk of spitting out a fan of crumbs, it would surely have been impolite for her to reply with anything more than a nod.

'As for me,' said the woman, 'I must say, both times it happened on day *two*. Burst into tears and found I was in love with what had been a bit of a squawking, mewling, nightmare little thing. Nurses told me: day two, normal. Most women fall in love with their babies on day *two*.'

My mother had by now swallowed her mouthful of cake, but still she merely nodded.

Cake, nothing, you ate the smell of lilac in that room.

'Once you know what it's about,' said the woman, 'second time around, God, you're oh so *very* much waiting for it to happen.'

~

I talked to Mrs Shaw. I listened to *Walkin'*. I came upstairs and messed about: *How wonderful, I thought, she's told me a story that ends with a perfect lie*, &c.

And then, no effort—no conscious effort—I switched tack and there I was, working. *Nature*, I wrote, and then, *resplendent in its diversity*, I searched my mind, *tops and tails the world with shimmering ice*.

What rubbish, *tops and tails* especially—*shimmering* also tremendously bad. It was the first dactyl that came to me, not that I specifically thought: *dactyl*.

I tried to generate a next sentence, but couldn't. It's impossible to avoid an advanced education in garbage, so usually I put myself in garbage mode, and garbage duly flows. But for once, the garbage side of my mind wasn't playing along.

The problem with this piece, I knew, was going to be the wish, the need, repeatedly to use the words 'frozen', 'icy' and 'ice'. If only 'gelid' looked as though it meant what it does mean, I thought, and if only 'frigid' weren't laden with sexual embarrassment. 'Glacial', 'arctic', 'polar', 'frosty': I might get away with any of these once; but 'frigid' or 'gelid' the subs would change without hesitation, and they'd whack in 'icy' instead, no doubt, causing the rhythm of the writing to fail, not that that would matter to anyone, and it happens that they always manage to do this anyway, so that I've given up looking at the courtesy magazines they send me, because text I am merely humiliated by when I email it to them I cannot bear when they post it back, wrecked, house-style.

I hadn't completed my researches at the library, but that was just an excuse now. Now I had to get on and write. But *shimmering*: dear oh dear. I try to solve these problems as I go along. I left that one pending because I simply couldn't think what to use instead.

In the polar wastelands, I continued, at last, *weird sculptures are constantly being thrown up by the clashing of ice plates*— sheets?—*but when human beings make ice sculptures*—at which I stalled again, thinking solely in expletives.

After a pause, I read out loud, '*In the polar wastelands, weird sculptures are constantly being thrown up by the clashing of ice sheets, but when human beings make ice sculptures,*' I needed another coffee, 'blank blank blank *between the inherent beauty of the medium, and*—' And somehow, because at last I had started to work, I felt safe to stop again. I really needed a coffee. I decided to go to the Minimart to get in supplies. The milk was finished as well: milk, coffee, bread. I had thought to give myself a day off from going out, but there's a limit.

I checked my purse for money, reflecting that this would not be the time to get myself dropped by my employers. I couldn't afford to become 'recalibrated personnel' or whatever they'd call it, just because of the ice piece. If the writing was going to be beyond shoddy, I thought, it would still be extra-nice pictures, wouldn't it?

As I wound slowly down the stairs, Edward Lloyd popped back into my mind. Might I really study him one day, even try to write a book about him? Wow, I thought—cheerful beyond reason as I considered his dates—it wouldn't be that hard to come up with the usual kinds of proofs to show that *he* had been Jack the Ripper!

Lloyd knew about *nice pictures*. In fact it was his understanding of this subject that led him to devise a delightfully neat way round the impediment of being legally compelled to print only lies. Just because his texts had to be fake news, it didn't mean he was barred from providing illustrations of stories that were real.

Mostly he stuck to a hit parade of recent murders, though one in five of his engravings showed a nautical disaster: a collision in harbour, CONFLAGRATION ON DECK, a steamer swamped, or CATASTROPHIC LOSS OF LIFE AMONGST SLAVES IN THE HOLD— Lloyd was an abolitionist. On one front page, he went so far as to depict the INHUMAN EXECUTION of a gang of pirates, each suspended, by iron hooks caught under the ribs, from a floating gallows off the coast of Russia.

Lloyd expressed nothing but contempt for the 'filthy abuse and low blackguardism' of those newspaper editors who paid to report genuine stories. He also pretended to despise the stories themselves. 'Were we ever so disposed to make observations upon the passing events of the day,' he noted airily, 'we are very well pleased with our present position; for there is nothing of any importance passing in the world to call for observation.' He could afford to adopt this tone. Somewhere around issue 23 of his paper, circulation figures rose above 100,000. 'Yes, reader,' he said, 'this is positively our sale.'

But he did sometimes crack. Even for a man prepared to illustrate a cat chewing the face off a nun, could anything rival the enormity of a real-life assassination attempt on Queen Victoria *pregnant*? Lloyd waited just eleven days after this event, until the 21st of June, 1840, to supply his readership with a massive engraving of the scene.

By the 21st of June, text was redundant anyway. Everyone knew what had happened. Lloyd risked merely a brief past-history of the would-be killer, Edward Oxford, who had been a 'froward' boy, fond of knives, liable to temper, &c.

Besides this guff—who knows, it may have been true—Lloyd also slipped a few words on the scandal into his leader column, though with legally advisable and, it has to be said, refreshing helplessness, he managed to supply not an iota of information. 'What motive could have induced the base assassin to commit such a diabolical outrage on his sovereign, we are perfectly at a loss to conceive.'

ATTEMPTED ASSASSINATION OF HER MAJESTY AND PRINCE ALBERT.

It does occasionally cross my mind that if I were required, for some reason I haven't yet invented, to provoke wide-scale bourgeois disquiet in England as it is today, one of my first orders to my minions would be to put an axe through the glass plate of every photocopy machine in the land. The average high-street photocopy machine has a so-called 'duty-cycle' of 60,000 copies per month. Any spare minions I'd have stick around with me, and together we'd foment a plan for blowing up all the depots everywhere that are used to store cartridges of ink.

The Minimart was busy. Nobody likes a cripple in a crowded supermarket. I heard a woman behind me mutter, 'Oh for God's sake.'

Myself, I was thinking what an extraordinary number of products have packaging dominated by images of athletic females. Breakfast cereals lead the way in this regard. I had been considering buying myself some cereal as an all-round food item, but, faced with the packaging, decided not to: a futile gesture of revolt.

Where has the *Big Issue* man got to? His pitch outside the Minimart has been vacant for days. It's not that someone else has muscled in on him. We usually pass a little time together. I don't know, it may be, as Con's father believes, that it's an intelligent insurance policy to cultivate a taste for wrecks and ruins, but if they have it in them to get drunk and disappear, you're liable to disappointment.

I made my way back up the stairs with my shopping hanging in front of me in my bag: coffee, soup, bread, butter. Only when I was most of the way up did it strike me that I'd forgotten to buy some milk.

Presumably even a person with legs in sensible working order would have baulked at turning round and going straight back down again. Enough was enough. Once was enough.

*

Wednesday

There was a message on the answer machine. I walked straight past it when I came into the flat, plus coffee, minus milk; but after a minute or two, with what is becoming customary nervousness, I pressed the button. 'Hiya. Archie. Just calling to say, bevvies at The Feathers tonight? Sevenish? I'm ringing round. Cheers. If not—Friday? Give me a call. Cheers.'

I am informed, I can't say reliably, but I am *informed* that my path to salvation will lie in making my own friends. That's a nice idea. It's one to think about. I'll definitely give that one a bit of a think. Oh sure—why not?

The way things are, I'm forced to consider that perhaps Archie no longer qualifies. This is not to overlook the fact that I have known him exactly the same length of time I've known my husband, less about a week; but I suppose now lines will be drawn.

Archie is a cellist. We have plenty to talk about. He likes books. Over time, he's lent me a number and given me two. And his brother, Malcolm, is a vet. It was Archie's brother who, one night, because I asked, told me what I know about diseases of the pigeon.

I stood there accepting that I could no longer take Archie's message as being by extension for me, whatever he'd thought when he left it. I felt out of control, the more so when I noticed that Mrs Shaw's hairspray was still on the book shelves. I laughed at the idea of using it on myself.

I'm waiting for something—*what*? The question slipped back into my mind.

I made a pot of coffee.

Alphonso Ramble had disorderly hair. So did my father; but

Alphonso—it's odd to think about this—was brought up with numerous servants, indoor and outdoor, gardeners and so on, plus yet other people who visited, like the clock winder, the knife grinder, and Mr Starling who cut the gentlemen's hair.

Mr Starling did this across several generations. Alphonso liked the system, and the two of them were fast friends from the start, and when Alphonso grew up, he became Mr Starling's doctor, which made no difference.

When Mr Starling died, Alphonso visited Mrs Starling in her council house on the edge of town. She was by then partially sighted, otherwise known as half blind. Alphonso proposed that she take over as his barber, and decreed that, as part of the revised arrangement, he would come to her place rather than vice versa. This could have been interpreted as a double act of kindness: Mrs Starling gets a regular visitor, and a little money to boot. But Alphonso said simply, 'I'm used to a member of the Starling family cutting my hair.'

Under the new regime, *Doctor*, who had always been a dapper man, began to look unkempt and thus a little sad. I don't think he minded overmuch. Stella Ramble minded.

A woman at Alphonso's funeral said to me that he had had a soft spot for all his patients. 'That man, your grandfather,' she said, 'a heart like butter.'

The vicar made the same point. 'Dr Alphonso Ramble,' he remarked ruefully, 'didn't give up on anyone. He wasn't a church-goer until the end of his life, and I don't believe he underwent a late access of faith. No. The explanation was something else: the Intercessions. Once he was forced to retire, I'm morally certain he came to church to keep tabs on who was sick and dying. Did he pray for his old patients? I think he walked out of church every Sunday with a list in his pocket of the people he needed to see. I know he did. Was he a good Christian? I leave this question to the Almighty, who are we—' &c. &c.

Alphonso was lauded at his death as a man who hadn't given up on anybody, not his barber's widow, no one.

And what of Stella Ramble, Alphonso's wife, she who had neither wished to know nor felt compelled to discover whether *Papa*—with whom she had wandered Berlin's Tiergarten for a year, and in whose chauffeur-driven Maybach she had swept through the city—whether her courtly Jewish *Papa* had survived the war?

What of Stella Ramble, who could throw out that 'one didn't go into that sort of thing'?

I have come to ask myself whether her complete disregard for the shape of a human life might not help to explain her difficulty in loving the man she took for a husband.

I sat down with a cup of black coffee and tried again to work:

Nature, resplendent in its diversity, tops and tails the world with shimmering ice. In the polar wastelands, weird sculptures are constantly being thrown up by the clashing of ice sheets, but when human beings make ice sculptures, — — — between the inherent beauty of the medium, and the—

And the defeating thing was—I thumped the table—I'd used 'ice' three times already. For some reason I hankered to write the 'vasty' polar wastelands.

I was out of time. I drank down my bitter coffee and made

myself write the rest of the article, made myself do it. I talked about how ice festival organisers mimic the Northern Lights with night-time displays of neon. I made that up. I mentioned the ice slides you can slide down and the hot tubs in Japan where you can warm up. I padded the thing with Manchu ice lanterns and discussed the aesthetics of the carvings, but not much because I was too weary to make the effort. Construction challenges proved more profitable. With construction challenges, I got into my stride. I blithered; I generated copy, Palace of Westminster inexplicably popular—why does 'copy' refer both to the original and its replica? Do I care? Perhaps not. As the word count creepingly grew, I observed, to my relief, that I was beyond question clocking up *nice pictures*.

I began to hanker for a little more caffeine to help me get the stupid thing right.

~

There is considerable space given over in my mind to facts that aren't true. One of them concerns the young gentlemen who went from England to Europe on the Grand Tour a century and more back. I have it that they would carry with them an item looking like a largish, rectangular magnifying glass, the glass itself being yellow and set in an ornate frame. These young men, in my head at least, were so foppishly enamoured of ancient paintings that, whenever they were confronted by a ravishing landscape, they would whip out one of these devices and improve their view with an illusory layer of degraded varnish.

When I found myself staring out of the window wishing I had one of these things, so that the limping pigeons would look more glamorous, I decided it was time for proper food.

On my way to the kitchen I had an impulse not to stop but to go all the way down to Mrs Shaw's flat to say, what had she meant by asking me so many questions?

Is it normal to be so enquiring? I felt I wanted to go downstairs and tell her: look, the reason I haven't spoken to my mother is that there'd be no earthly use. It doesn't work. For example, when my father died, I asked her what they'd been talking about before he fell down the stairs.

She said, 'We were talking about you.'

I said, 'What about me?'

She said, 'He was in a stew about—what should we do about you.'

I said, 'What are you on about?'

She said, 'He was worried about you.'

'He was?'

'Yes.'

'He was?'

'He wanted to know if he should do anything.'

'He came to you about this?'

'Yes.'

'I don't understand. Why did he ask you? What did you say?'

'I'm your mother,' she burst out crossly. 'Why wouldn't he ask me?'

'But I don't understand. What was he in a stew about?'

'I don't know, your fly-by-night wedding, and then you don't

seem to be getting on with anything. I mean, you're so rude,'
she said, 'no one knows what to think.'

'What did you say when he said he was worried?'

'Oh, we had a little chat,' she adopted the tone of someone
explaining the changing of the guard to a foreigner, 'and I told
him I thought you were the type of person who likes to plough
their own furrow, if he hadn't noticed.'

'So?' I said.

'Well, it's obvious. You're young. You make your own
mistakes. We all do.'

'That's what you said? What did he say?'

She paused—for effect, I thought at first—but then, as
though she really meant it, said, 'Poor little mite.'

I felt ill. 'Are you saying, *yourself*,' I asked her, '"poor little
mite", or are you telling me he said it?' I felt ill, the more so
when I saw that I'd lost her.

She gazed around breathing through her nose. 'Six o'clock
I think. Fancy one?'

Anyway, screw that. I didn't go downstairs to Mrs Shaw, I sat
in the kitchen and ate some bread and butter.

My last meal with Con, tinned sardines and oranges: still
nauseating to think of. When I married him, I was pleased to
be able to hide in the noise of his life. I wanted to. Then, last
year, he stopped playing me his music. But this only made
the noise of him seem louder and I didn't so much like it any
more. I don't really know what I'm saying, except that a plate
of bread and butter by myself was restful, I noticed, no matter
that it was hard to eat because I wasn't hungry.

Near the end of his spiel, he said, 'Half the time I don't

know what you're thinking, half the time I don't give a shit and half the time I don't believe you're thinking anything anyway.'

This was the only point in his speech where I had a strong yen to concur, though in retrospect his comment strikes me as annoying.

I stared at my plate and imagined the flat being on fire and wondered: if I could take only what I was able to fit in my bike-messenger bag, what would I take—books, knickers, toothbrush? But the flat wasn't on fire. I didn't really feel I belonged, and couldn't think what I was doing there sitting eating.

After my bread and butter the evening lagged, and by nightfall any trace of restfulness was extinguished by quiet panic. My stomach hurt. I didn't know what to do about it and found myself diverted sideways into—it came to me like this: *think about it*, Mrs Shaw is married to a crook, and she's irregular herself; well, in some ways—not as to folding blankets, it has to be admitted; but consider whether you haven't underestimated her. Forget Goldilocks and the porridge, perhaps none of what she's told you has been true.

I thought about this and worried about it as I went to bed.

Only when I was lying down did I observe that I had chosen to sleep in the bed despite the sofa being categorically free. Well, I hadn't chosen it. I'd just gone to bed.

I stayed where I was and thought and worried, at the same time telling myself that Mrs Shaw's business was nothing to do with me, I was making it up, and it didn't matter anyway. I was distracted by the approach of a girl below on the street, who wailed with tiresome, alcoholic mournfulness. We get a lot of night trouble round here. I think she sat down right on our front wall. She began a plaint of the order, 'I can't take it, it's too much, I've had it up to here, leave me alone, no no no.'

The boy who was with her responded along the lines of, 'Pull yourself together, get a grip, shut your trap, what's your problem *now*?'

In my head I supplied them—I couldn't help myself—with a jaundiced bass line: *such is life, you win some you lose some, it'll all look better in the morning, worse things have happened at sea.*

Though I hadn't been anything like close to falling asleep, I lay there and resented the fact that the boy and the girl were keeping me awake.

When at last they wandered off, I found my worries had clarified somewhat. My panic was wrapped up in Mrs Shaw's having told me one of the tidiest stories I've ever heard. Perhaps I had been wrong to imagine she'd had to dredge around in her mind to remember it. Perhaps, during her interlude with the cigarette, she had been debating with herself whether I sufficiently deserved to be told anything so very finely tuned.

If that was it, I thought, if she was exceptionally good at this kind of thing, did it not follow that every word she'd said to me about credit cards, pick-pocketing and meters could have been a sell? Might she not have been winging it each time, hoping my husband really had left me, and wouldn't come back; really had disappeared and gone silent, as, repeatedly, I had confirmed?

Her husband, according to her, strayed off on Saturday in

search of funds. Their discount, under-the-table, fortnight's rent was apparently owing on Tuesday morning. 'Right, two weeks yesterday we been here.'

What had she planned to do if Mr Shaw didn't get back in time to pay? Had she been giving herself the option of being able to bang on my door and say to me that my amateur of a husband, off thieving with hers—my husband still technically my husband—had screwed up big time, in Brighton, say, compromising others, say, and that, cutting all the crap, it now fell to me to get him out of it?

Suppose every word of what she'd said to me had been a set up, and I—somehow—suppose I'd found the required money? How easily she could have pretended to me that she was off to Brighton to square things, and that as a gimpy-legged cripple I must hand her the cash and watch her walk away.

I'm still thinking about this. As stories go, is it not ship-shape? Is it not at least a *possibility*, for a person of Mrs Shaw's fabulously high standards? Am I wrong? Is this me?

I did see that if there was any truth to it, there was a further point to consider, namely, that—who knows why—if she'd started out by setting me up, she'd ended by choosing to spare me.

The thought of her with Mr Harbottle was worse than Bobbo's soaps. I shivered again at the sense of it I've been carrying in my mind.

With all of this, and for every other piled-up reason, I lay in a heap feeling trashed. Then, right there, abruptly and simply, I was struck by an electric insight.

I knew what it was I'd been waiting for—had been, was and still am. It oughtn't to have been a revelation but it was.

I am waiting, with, now, a peculiar sort of excitement, to find out *what happens next*.

6

Thursday

I got up early. I'd slept quite well, despite 'I can't take it', 'get a grip', &c., and felt better than for some time. I decided when I woke that, barring accidents, today I would definitely visit Stella Ramble.

The pigeons are back pacing the sills opposite on their tottery, garbled feet. Why are so many of them lame?

Re the morning, I can't think. I tried to catch up on things, until it wasn't morning any more. I do remember I spent some time dreaming about how much I would have liked to be the particular clerk in the Stamp Office who was required to read through Edward Lloyd's fake newspapers to confirm he hadn't printed anything true, knowing that if I found Lloyd out, my superiors would haul him up before the courts. Compared to normal work, what incredible fun, and how thrilling.

If I had detected a bona fide news item, would Lloyd have been required to say, 'I promise to tell the truth, the whole—' &c. &c.?

I concede that life for a clerk in 1840s London was grim.

They were bullied, starved, slowly blinded and so on, besides which, you didn't get to be one if you were a woman; though is there any point feeling indignant about that now? English women didn't get to be clerks until the 1890s, with mass production of the typewriter; and even then, to get a clerking job they had to be unmarried. Ah.

That poor Stamp Office clerk, though, the last thing he would have read in each issue of Lloyd's paper, at the bottom of the last column on the last page, was an advertisement for the Medical Institution, No. 1 Brunswick Cottages, Brunswick Street, Hackney Road, London. The list of ailments curable not only varied week by week, but their number depended on the amount of space that needed filling, at the discretion of the typesetter: a convenient arrangement. But no matter what's on it, this list always reads as a sort of hypochondriac's charter, hypochondria being just about the only problem that doesn't get a mention. You could choose from,

Nervous or Mental Disorders, Loss of Hearing, Noises in the Head, and Discharges of the Ear, Scurvy, Impurities of the Blood, and Defects of the Skin, and Nervous Complaints, attended with Lowness of Spirits, Anxiety, Sense of Fear, Palpitation of the Heart, Trembling, Melancholy, Despair, Irresolution, Diffidence, Languor, Exhaustion, Defective Memory and Sight, Indigestion, Loss of Appetite, Heartburn, Giddiness, Nausea, Cramp, Weakness, Lumbago, Palsy, Spasms, Fits, Piles, Worms, &c.

Whatever the list, in any given week surely a normal person would have suffered at least half the diseases on offer? If you applied personally, or by letter, prepaid, they undertook to supply proofs of 'the most deplorable nervous cures'.

~

I decided to do a short stint in the library before catching a bus to the old people's home. As I got myself down the bottom flight of stairs, Mrs Shaw stepped out of her flat, closed the door behind her and immediately lounged against the hall wall, smoking.

'Hi,' I said.

She blew out and whispered, 'There's something I would've told you, all right, but I promised.'

Wonderful, I thought.

'You'll figure it out,' she said.

'All right.' Sympathetically, I whispered in reply.

She flicked her ash onto the floor. 'Meter okay?'

'I don't know. I suppose so. I mean—yes, presumably.'

There was a long pause, then she pointed at my lower half with her cigarette. 'How's the legs?'

'They are as they are. Not bad, for me.'

'That's it then. Hey, that Harbottle,' Mrs Shaw laughed a locked-down version of her growly, dirty laugh; almost inaudibly, she breathed, *'prick like a lever handle.'*

I couldn't resist smiling.

She flicked her ash again, said, 'Bloody hell,' sighed and then said, 'So you stick up for yourself, you know. Sort your head out a little bit previous next time you're, right, in trouble, whatever, so they can't get you, you know?'

'Okay,' I said. Why *were* we whispering? 'Perhaps you and

I could have a beer again some evening, if your husband's ever off again? I owe you a drink, no?'

She stuck out her left hand to show me her diamond ring. 'Know what it's worth?'

I shook my head. I didn't, in any dimension, know what it was worth.

'Shop-bought brand new,' she said, as though that was in its favour.

Fair enough.

I could have spent hours rewriting the ice piece, but I typed it up on one of the library computers and sent it off under a strict charge to myself not to make a single improvement. This took some restraint. I was cushioned from minding too much about the collapse of my already-collapsed standards by receiving a message from Beata.

Dear Ramble,

Thank you most sincerely for your help with my letter. I am fed up with this business and Professor Cohen has just gone to Samos for a week, an aspect of which I was not aware. I am just worried the library board wants me to deceive for them. What a problem when I have important work to do.

Boustrophedon is when the lines of the inscription go left to right, right to left (retrograde means the characters being r to l too as in a mirror), left to right etc. Boustrophedon translates to mean the way oxen turn back and forth over a field when they plough. Whereas, false boustrophedon, alternate lines instead of having vertical orientation will curl round upside down, this also being called Schlangenschrift which means snake-writing. There are yet more variants but that is all you need to know. These archaic folk made things quite accurate, but in fragments it is no good and often the stonemasons got it wrong as they didn't understand. Spolia is when they used pieces of old constructions to make new ones, recycling you might say, so you might find some fragments of archaic inscriptions in the walls of a Byzantine chapel for example. A squeeze is when you take for example wet filter paper and press it over an inscription cut in stone to take a 3d copy. I should have remembered to explain you all of this because of course you asked!

When are you going to start studying again, about anything?

Bea.

I replied:

Cheers. Thanks for filling me in. I'm tempted to make a joke about what your main squeeze is. If that doesn't make sense, don't worry. If an English girl ever talks to you about squeezing her lemon, she means she's got to have a pee. A man might say he needed to water his horse. Anyway, I'm off the point. I realise I forgot to answer your question about anonymous and accredited. Do you want to send me the sentence in question? I'm happy, as ever, to check it for you.

I'm sorry you are in a snarl with your library people. I like the sound of Marfleet's fairly worthless squeezes. Perhaps they could be used for an art installation? Again, I'm joking.

Best, Ramble.

Over time, I have learnt that it is better to insult Beata's intelligence by flagging when I'm being silly than to leave her with a margin of doubt.

I knew I wanted to talk to Stella Ramble but felt increasingly anxious on the bus. What I didn't know was what I thought talking would achieve. There's hardly anything left in her mind.

Was I—this possibility made me contemplate turning back—was I setting myself up for more distress of the kind I associate with the hat-shop photograph?

When I saw that her memory had started to collapse I felt disturbed—had an unpleasant feeling about the shape of *her* life: that it had been washed overboard, that I was too late to save it. I tired her out with questions she couldn't answer. The hat-shop photograph—she never managed to explain anything about it, why she'd had it, and kept it; what it had meant to her. She simply didn't know. This was intolerable to me, though I saw that, in the abstract, there was a defeating sort of value to this transaction between us: her being unable to remember was something I couldn't myself forget.

This defeat, as I say, made me all the more determined to find out what she had meant by 'Fuesenberg'. The first time I had tried to pursue this on the Web, I'd not only drawn a blank, but had found myself slowed, as one is slowed by extreme coldness, as I searched through the sites I did discover—gruesome sites, sites in languages I couldn't determine, hideous sites for the collectors of special-issue stamps found on letters posted out of the concentration camps: *nice pictures*.

In time, though, I pulled together enough clues to work it

out, I think. 1929, an expensive lunatic asylum in 'Fuesenberg', possibly north of Berlin: I became convinced that Stella Ramble had been trying to say *Fürstenberg*. Fürstenberg, N. of Berlin, was, then, a small town in a beautifully forested area destined to be littered with the Ravensbrück subcamps. The one concentration camp besides Ravensbrück that was close to Berlin was Sachsenhausen. Stella Ramble had surely been meaning Fürstenberg, on the rail line for those being taken to Ravensbrück. From what I could gather, the place where she had stayed had become a part of the one camp designated women-only, though male infants were sent in with their mothers, or were born inside.

Ravensbrück was classed by those who ran it as merely a concentration camp, not a death camp, but thousands upon thousands upon thousands there were killed.

Stella Ramble had casually fixed in my mind the image of her Jewish *Papa*'s mad wife running through the forest in 1929, gripped by mortal terror. Viewed through the shadows that fell soon after, she did not appear to me so very lunatic.

The Berlin book, *Papa*'s gift, has an introduction, a *geleitwort*, by Alfred Döblin. It's a photograph book. It came out in the same year as Döblin's own landmark German Expressionist novel, *Berlin Alexanderplatz*. I take it *Papa* was a cultured man, and that he gave Stella Ramble photographs because, after all their nattering in the Tiergarten, he grasped that his English girl was suitably uneducated for her station in life and wasn't inclined to read, even in her own language. If he wished her to remember Berlin, she might at least look at these photographs, whatever she saw in them.

My favourite shot has the caption, 'Pietons, Die Fußgänger, Pedestrians'. It's as though you are *required* to stare at the people in it, and I like to fancy that it is Stella Ramble herself, in a jaunty hat, snapped by von Bucovich at the beginning of her visit, who is the right-most mark on the street. In such a form she may be enshrined, perceptibly of her era and no less real for seeming imprecise.

I returned to this picture several times, compelled by it, until one day I noticed that the pedestrians had been strolling in line with their own shadows. It then struck me that the camera, way up, had also been just about in line, though not in the same part of the sky as the sun. From the 1840s onwards, photographs were popularly called 'sun-pictures', as though the sun itself had been their author. But this shot is taken from the shadow side. If what we are seeing is late morning, then the photograph has been taken from somewhere in the afternoon, and if the afternoon, then from somewhere late in the morning. A person who knew what month this was, and the axis of the street, could read the pedestrians as a disorganised shoal of sundials; but simply labelled, *Die Fußgänger, Berlin*, the time they are telling is lost.

To my dismay, I arrived at the care home just after Mrs Marechal. Mrs Marechal is the only person besides me who still faithfully visits my grandmother, and she travels a distance to do so. Her visits are not regular. Occasionally we coincide.

Stella Ramble was sitting in her chair with a lidless lipstick in one hand and an open mirror compact in the other. You walk in and you're hit with the odour of urine.

'Stell,' said Mrs Marechal, 'just look at this girl—' waving at me. 'How are you Stell? How are you in the downstairs department? Any better? Look at this girl. Why the devil do you dress like that, Girly? What's your news anyway? Sit still, Stella. Look, I've heaved this chair all the way from reception. Are you all right sitting on the bed?'

'Yes, I'm fine,' I said.

'Do you want this chair?'

'No, I'm fine.'

'Sure?'

'I'm completely sure.'

'Because I just heaved it all the way from reception.'

'Please, you sit on it.'

'Your decision,' she said and sat on it. 'So, darling, how are your intimate regions? Any better? Let's have the television off.' Mrs Marechal got up again. 'So impossibly *hot* in here as well. I'll be sweating like the proverbial. Let's have a window. Might make a through-draught. I always say, I'm a great believer in draughts. Open the door—window: phewph.'

'Sherry?' said Stella Ramble.

I had put a box of chocolates in front of her on her tray table. 'How about a chocolate?' I said.

'Oh quite right,' said Mrs Marechal, 'quite right. Start on the sherry, nurses'll be down on us like a ton of bricks. Have you seen the new lady who's running this dive? New lady, Stell.'

Stella Ramble offered Mrs Marechal a chocolate. 'Take two, save yourself a journey.'

'Nummy nums. Don't mind if I do. Yes, she's gigantic.'

'I thought the new person didn't start until December,' I said, 'or is she just visiting?'

'Haven't the slightest. She was puffing about in reception. Introduced herself when I stole this chair. Clinically obese, I don't wonder. I should think she weighs, goodness, eighteen stone.'

I began to feel extremely concerned that Mrs Marechal might be overheard by someone walking along the corridor. She isn't exactly slim herself, though that doesn't have much to do with anything.

'But exquisitely dressed, all credit,' she said. 'Can't imagine where she gets her clothes. Doesn't look like the kind of fat women you see on trains, she looks like someone you might see getting into a taxi. I always think people like that usually lack all restraint and the food here is so stodgy. Stodgy food, Stella. Looks well on it though, doesn't she? Don't you, Stell. What was that stuff one used to give children to build them up? Not Minidex. What was it? Absolutely disgusting, slimy. Disgusting.'

'Rose hip syrup,' said Stella Ramble.

'No, no no, I've almost—*Angier's Emulsion*. Revolting stuff.'

'Revolting?' said Stella Ramble.

'Malt,' said Mrs Marechal. 'Don't get me started. Cod liver oil.'

'The Victorian poor used to have this stuff they gave their babies called Venice Treacle, which induced an opium stupor while the mothers went out to work.'

'You don't mean to tell me,' Mrs Marechal gave a great piping laugh, 'that the opium of the masses was *opium*?'

'Well, opium and gin perhaps; I don't know.'

'Gin and opium?' Stella Ramble spoke with the curious enthusiasm of one to whom this didn't sound half bad.

'Now, what about all these catalogues?' Mrs Marechal stood up again. 'I can't be doing with these. You don't want all these catalogues do you Stell?' She shuffled through them. 'Garden furniture? Thermals? In this place? Honest to goodness. Let's sling them and give you a bit of space.'

I thought: space for what?

'Don't get up, darling, Stell, Stella. Stella, sit down. I'll do it. What's the problem? Glory, who on earth did your hair? It's all squiffy at the back. Your grandmother used to be such a natty dresser and just look at her. Look at you both. What a pair—and you're not even bonkers, Girly.'

Usually when I visit Stella Ramble it's like sinking into

the carpet at The Admiral. A soft, dark intoxication under-
lies the mood. But Mrs Marechal was keeping us on edge.
Stella Ramble came out with the same fragile laugh each time
she picked up a cue: stole a chair! eighteen stone! ladies on
trains!

'You've been to Italy, Stell? Marvellous if I do say so. Point
being, go to Italy, fetch up at just about any hairdresser's and
they're so badly lit inside they're good as pitch black, so you
look in the mirror and you look wonderful before they even
begin and then you just look better and better. Then you come
back to Blighty and they have these terrible tube lights—strip
lights are they called?—anyway, you never look worse than in
the mirror at an English hairdresser's, especially when your
hair's still wet. Hideous. I suppose you're meant to go home
and think, hurrah, perhaps I don't look quite so awful after
all. Alphonso, now, I always thought, when they poled up
with his corpse at the undertaker's, funeral chappies must have
assumed death by electrocution. Never could understand such
a bantycock type of a man going to seed like that.'

I didn't know whether by 'bantycock type' she was meaning
Alphonso had been homosexual. Stella Ramble told me a
while ago—who knows what she was thinking—that after my
father was born, Alphonso had ceased to 'come into her life'.
Perhaps by 'bantycock type', Mrs Marechal simply meant a
bantycock type, whatever that is. I remember at Alphonso's
funeral, some woman said to me that my grandparents had
been a marvellous-looking couple, 'a feast for the eye'.
Something like four hundred people came to his funeral.

'How's that beastly husband of yours?' As soon as Mrs
Marechal had asked me this, she interrupted herself, 'I've

absolutely got to have another chocolate.' She had another chocolate. 'Gosh, rum truffle but more-so. Too good. But what a cold fish that boy is, don't you think, Stell? Girly here's married a cold fish, just like her father.'

I felt an urge to say something uncivil, except, did she mean that my father had been a cold fish, or that he—like me, in her opinion—had married one? I couldn't work it out. I have problems, sometimes, understanding what people mean. I think to myself, well, you're deaf; but sometimes I just can't work out how the words fit together.

'But what did I do?' Mrs Marechal asked eerily. 'Married a drinker, loved him to pieces, stuck him in the ground at forty-nine. Stell, if you don't stop wiggling—I say, this place might cream a hospital, but it's not much go as a hotel. Hope the new woman puts the heating down. She'll sweat, golly! Hope I die in my bed that's all I can say. Over and out. Stella, give her fifty quid so she can have a proper haircut.'

'Fifty!' I said.

'I seem to have lost my handbag.'

'I know. What's the use,' said Mrs Marechal to me. 'You'd do something hideous with a pair of nail scissors and spend the fifty on books.'

'Pointless,' I said.

'Now, now,' said Mrs Marechal.

'I can't seem to find my bag.'

'No, Stell, someone's looking after it for you.' To me, Mrs Marechal said, in a loudly suppressed voice, 'Tell Mr Hopp you want the money and Stell's agreed. I'll back you up.'

'I suppose I could.'

'Could but won't, I don't know, I give up. Do you know,

Hopp is also money man for another friend of mine, ninety-three, and he had the gall to tell her she should stop smoking. She's ninety-three! What's the matter with the man?' Mrs Marechal stood up. 'Flying visit. I'm expected.' She went back to her shouty quiet voice, 'Don't worry, she'll be going gang-busters for years to come.' Confidingly, she added, 'Bit of a chitter chat seems to perk her up no end, don't you think? Used to be such a gay bird, I can't tell you, a *gay young thing*— well, truth be told, a bit of a bad hat in her day.'

'Who was that?' asked Stella Ramble, pointing her finger vaguely round the room as though tracing the flight of a wasp.

'Mrs Marechal,' I said.

'Gas-bags.'

'Yes.'

'Tiring.'

'Yes. Strangely enough, I think her good side and her bad side are the same thing.'

'Oh dear.'

'I mean it was nice of her to throw away all your catalogues, but it was also somewhat interfering, don't you think? I remember Alphonso once called her a brute, and he wasn't often rude about anybody.'

'Why did she want a haircut?'

'She wanted me to have one.'

'You, darling?'

'Yes. She thinks I look shock-headed.' At once I felt that 'shock-headed' was probably not to do with electrocution, but with shocks of wheat.

'It's the fashion.'

'I'm touched you think so.'

'Do I know her?'

'You used to.'

With this, we settled into the easy slowness for which I'd been geared on arrival. Our conversation proceeded extra-ordinarily slowly. Stella Ramble's bedside clock ticked many times between our exchanges. I think we only just saved ourselves from losing track of what we were on about.

'I wish I had a darker lipstick.'

'Really?'

'I like this colour but I wouldn't say I adore it.'

'Are your other lipsticks in the bathroom?'

'I don't know. I'm a bit gaga.'

'I could look if you like.'

'A body could make herself a little bag for her lipsticks.'

I drifted:

First, rip one of your piss-stained dresses into handy squares of cloth. Then ask nurse to give you a sewing needle (don't be surprised if she says no). If all else fails, stick the cloth together with Sellotape, then stuff in your lipsticks any old way you can. Do not whimper as you perform this task, or nurse may seize the opportunity to ramp up your astonishing complement of drugs. Should the seams split, endeavour to control your shud-dering fingers in such a way as to—

'How are you, darling?'

'I'm fine.'

'What have you been up to?'

'More or less just mooching.'

'Are you quite sure?'

'That's all right, isn't it?'

'Oh yes, rather.'

'What about you?'

'I've been mooching too. I'm a bit dotty.'

'Don't worry about it.'

'I don't.'

'How's your old lady friend, who says hello sometimes?'

'I think she's popped off.'

'Oh.'

'People tend to do that around here.'

'Well, what about snagging one of the old gents—get yourself a boyfriend?'

'I would very much like a sort of tame duck to follow me around, but I don't know how to start something like that.'

'You don't?'

'I could have him in here all day.'

A helper, Sandra, put her head round the door, saw me, nodded and disappeared again.

Stella Ramble was surprised by this intrusion. She looked disconcerted and said imperiously, 'Where's the aeroplane?'

'The what?'

'I wish to speak to my granddaughter.'

'The telephone?'

'I can't remember how it works.'

I rocked up onto my feet, stretched over and gave her the phone, then sat back down and watched as she tried to call me. She was right that she couldn't remember how it worked.

*

Here's another Browning joke, printed in a London newspaper the year after he died:

> How to Read Browning: Miss Pert (who has given him a copy of Browning's poems): I declare, Mr. Cutely, you're holding that book upside down. Cutely (not an admirer of Browning): Yes, that's the proper way to read this book.

Forget the question of who this was aimed at, it's difficult to believe such a joke could ever have been deemed really tremendously funny.

I broke in on Stella Ramble's dream. I didn't know how to express myself so I imitated her. 'I'm afraid I have something rather beastly to tell you. I'm afraid I think I'm getting a divorce.'

'Oh no darling, don't,' she said, gazing at me with her washed blue eyes. 'Don't. You *must* weather it. There are too many divorces. You have a daughter to consider. Really don't do it. I know she's a little menace, but it's only larks. You shouldn't be always squashing her. You should be kind and talk to her more. You should talk to them both more. Middleton's always been tricky, I know it can't be easy, but Alphonso's always talked to me.'

Sandra came back in again. 'Hello there.'

'Hello,' I said.

'Hello Mrs Ramble. It's tea. Tea now, pet? Ready for tea?'

'Jolly good,' said Stella Ramble. She used to drink a vile type of tea that smelled like a gas leak. If I had any idea of its name, I'd bring her some, but I hate all tea, didn't think about

it at the time, and now I don't remember. She's never understood the word 'tea' as used to mean supper, so she made no
move to get up.

I did get up. I rose to my feet and leant awkwardly over
her to kiss her goodbye. Had I really been a little menace?

'What's the matter with your legs?'

'I'm all right.'

'Do they trouble you?'

'I'm all right. It looks worse than it is. I'm fine. Hey, why
are legs funny?'

'I beg your pardon?'

'I'm telling you a joke.'

'Oh. I can't remember what you said.'

'Why are legs funny?'

'I don't know, darling.'

'Here's the joke: Why are legs funny? *Because the bottom's
at the top.*'

After a slight pause, Stella Ramble started to laugh—a real,
unaffected, merry laugh. She only quenched it in order to be
able to say, 'Leaving so soon, darling?'

'You'll find I've gone, and then I'll just turn up again,' I said.

'Like a bad penny,' said Stella Ramble, and she smiled at
me beatifically.

I lugged the extra chair back to reception, then signed the
sign-out book. You have to put the time down. It was twenty
past five.

In the matter of bad jokes, the repressive view is well put by
Christina Rossetti, who wrote, in 1885: 'Can a pun profit?
Seldom I fear. Puns and such like are a frivolous crew likely

to misbehave unless kept within strict bounds.' Strict bounds on a pun? As Charles Lamb put it, several decades earlier, a pun is, 'an antic which does not stand upon manners'. Rossetti must have been dismayed by the jokes of her own era. 'What part of speech is required when you kiss?—To kiss requires *conjugation*, but Miss must *decline*.'

How she would have despised the only item I did inherit from the Bangalore Torpedo, a joke that came to me via my mother. Whenever anyone used a word like 'pseudonym' or 'psychoactive', it was, I gather, her habit to shrill, 'The P is silent, as in *bath*.'

As for Mrs Marechal saying 'gangbusters'—where does that come from?

To be alone, I was forced into a seat above the rear wheels of the bus, and suffered each time the driver went over an irregularity in the road. I thought about moving but couldn't be bothered. The floor of the bus was spotted with ancient, cloud-coloured, flattened gobs of gum. I hope Stella Ramble dies in her sleep, over and out; but I don't want it to happen specially soon. *DNR. Gangbusters.*

She won't be remembered, I thought, unless, by some brilliant mischance, following a near-fatal infection or broken hip, she manages, say, to plunge down a hospital lift shaft. She'd need something on a par with being eaten by an alligator. After a wasted life like hers, she'd need to sever her arteries walking through a plate-glass door, to be squashed to death by a horse, or to be struck by asteroid detritus. She'd need a *shockingly shattered head*. I happen to know that falling down the stairs isn't good enough; but animals, asteroids or pints and pints of blood would all be good lines to pursue.

Nevertheless, myself, I'd prefer that she go like Alphonso, in her sleep, without fuss; though perhaps he did fuss, who knows? As far as I'm aware, nobody. Stella Ramble wasn't there. Alphonso died in bed while Stella Ramble was away on a serene coach tour experience of classic wold-type settings in the Cotswolds.

It has occurred to me that her life is slowly being compressed, is being shrunk, constrained and restricted to an unmediated present tense, as a form of retribution, because of her ruthless disrespect for people's endings. The trouble with this theory is that she isn't sufficiently, or even *at all*, unhappy.

I got off the bus, upset, and there was Johnson. He was wearing a grass-green cotton duster coat with the most enormous buttons down the front: 'natty', as Mrs Marechal would say.

'Where have you been?' He sounded peeved.

'I don't know, where have you been?'

'Hole in the Wall.'

'Oh. I've just been seeing Stella Ramble. We don't have a plan, do we?'

'Of course we do.'

I found myself glancing through the window of The Hole in the Wall as though I might catch sight of Johnson inside. 'I'm—did we fix something? I don't remember fixing anything. I thought you said you'd phone me.'

'What?'

'I'm terribly sorry. I don't know what's the matter with me. She's, she's beginning to forget how the telephone works. She has to get help with it. She sat there with me in the room

182

trying to phone me up, I mean I was there and, or *but*, she was trying to phone me up and she couldn't even figure out the buttons.'

'One more thing.'

'Yes, and not a small one-more-thing, if she can't phone me without help. She's—how long have you been waiting? Hey,' I said, 'are you a "bantycock type"?'

'Am I a *what*? Ramble? I just ate an early supper through sheer boredom, that's how long I've been waiting, darling: omelette, chips, beans, ketchup on everything. I rang your doorbell, but Con and you weren't there. I wish you'd get a mobile.'

'I don't need one, really I don't. That sounds very yellowy, orangey, red. You didn't have marrowfat peas or something? Sorry I messed up. Would you like to come up for a coffee? You never come up to the flat. Don't worry, Con isn't around right now. Come to think of it, I've got to get some milk at the Minimart. I've been drinking pints of coffee lately. I've been writing a lot. I'm so sorry I forgot the plan. I so completely forgot it, I feel like you're making it up when you say we had one. I don't mean I don't believe you, I just don't remember anything about it.'

'Don't worry,' he said. 'Don't you worry. I'll do the worrying. First things first, have you eaten?'

'Yes,' I said—but vacantly, to acknowledge that I'd heard the question.

I was picturing Johnson standing, confused, outside the building where I live. How could I possibly have forgotten him twice in one week? I could think of no precedent for my neglecting him in this way. What had he thought when there was no answer? Had he stood there long?

When my pelvic ligament began to deteriorate, I was forced to answer rings on the doorbell by calling down out of the window, 'Can I help you? Up here! Hello?'

I got used to this. If it turned out to be something promising, I learnt to yell, 'Do you think you could wait, I'm slow on my legs, okay; or could you just leave it there for me? I'm on my way down.' If it was someone in the grip of religion, or an ex-prisoner selling dish cloths, I didn't go down. Keep your religion, I'd think to myself, keep your dish cloths.

I took to throwing my keys out of the window. There's a narrow strip of garden in front of the building, left as scrub. It isn't that I risk hitting a passer-by. But Johnson's last visit to the flat pre-dated all this. How long had he waited for me to show up at the door, thinking I should be there?

I was tired from my expedition, was slow even for me. Johnson said, 'I'll pop in and get the milk. You wait here.' I leant against the glass front of the Minimart while he bought milk.

Once I'd let us into my building, Johnson said, 'Give me the keys. I'll go on up ahead, yes? And put the kettle on?'

I got myself up the stairs thinking about the size of houses. I used to stay with my piano-tuner grandfather for half terms. We'd go tuning together, but we always also fitted in a boating trip. One time we planned to have a boating picnic after a morning visit to a new piano that wasn't so far away from the boating lake. Every meal was more or less a picnic with my grandfather anyway. He didn't cook. We used to have toast, baked beans, apples and tinned plum tomatoes, the peeled ones, which he called 'elephant's afterbirth'; there was railway cake with glacé cherries in it; we ate tinned mandarin segments, marmite sandwiches, all sorts of good things; but whatever we ate, we always ended with a piece of cheese. Grandfather would say, at the end of every meal, 'Have a piece of cheese to take the taste away.'

We found the place we were looking for. The building was tiny, a two up, two down in a long terrace of identical houses, with a single window on the ground and on the upper floor, and the front door flush to the pavement. Grandfather rang the bell.

The man who showed us in was muttering furiously. 'You live in a big house, people wait at your door. They ring the bell and wait. You live in a small house, they ring the bell and start walking. At once they walk away. Your house is small. Why should it take you two minutes to reach the front door?'

'Fair enough,' said Grandfather. Although he and I had meekly stood and waited, it felt as though we somehow hadn't.

I remember that the muttering man had a Bosendorfer grand that took up practically the whole of his front room, which you walked into right off the street.

'Bosendorfer,' said Grandfather afterwards. 'Good as a Steinway, give or take. How he got it in without a sledge-hammer, I'll never know.'

When I was small, I innocently thought that people who were angry were more likely than calm people to be correct about whatever it was they were saying. As we drove to the lake—I absolutely loved boating, Grandfather always called me Madam when we were on the lake: he loved it too—I asked whether it was true that people never waited when they rang the bell on little houses.

Grandfather replied that when he'd been a child, a house like that might have had ten children in it. 'People don't think nowadays,' he said, 'but back then it wasn't just, the more kids you had, the less space there was. The more kids you had, the more of your dough you needed for food and necessaries, the less there was for the rent. So the more kids you had, thing is, you had to keep moving into smaller and smaller houses.'

When finally I got up to the flat, I felt the force of knowing that someone I care about was waiting for me.

Johnson and I sat together in the kitchen. He had tea and I had coffee.

'How's the book shop?' I asked.

'Yea annoying, frankly. They're all fussed about the humidity levels. Humidity? Let's talk about something else, I'm fed up with it.'

'Okay.'

'Oh yes, but I have to tell you something totally funny.'

'Go on then.'

'Well, in the shop—this old lady, I didn't swerve away fast enough and she trod on my foot, so I said, "Excuse me!" And she said, "What?" And I said, "Well, you just trod on my foot." And she said—what do you think she said?'

'I don't know. I can't imagine.'

'She said, "Oh yes? *Prove it.*"'

At first Johnson and I just laughed. Then we really laughed.

'Cracked!' he said.

'Prove it?'

'Yes: "Oh yes? *Prove it.*"'

'I must remember that.'

There was a lull, then Johnson said, 'A what?—a *bantycock* type? What?'

'One of Stella Ramble's friends was there and she described Alphonso as having been a "bantycock type". I didn't know if that meant that he was gay, that's why I asked. Middleton thought he might have been, because of Stella Ramble having an affair for years and years and Alphonso doing nothing about it, plus I don't know what else. It doesn't really matter any more, and nobody knows the answer anyway, or nobody knows that I'm aware. You know, when my grandparents married, I mean during actually getting married, during the vows, Stella Ramble crossed her fingers behind her back in full view of the entire congregation and nobody said a word.'

'Come on.'

'She did. She absolutely did. In her own way she was quite daring.'

'Do you know how my father found out about me?'

I answered Johnson with a look, to say: I don't know.

'In fact he hit me,' Johnson said. 'He caught me kissing Oliver Hassan in my bedroom. But I think he knew already. He cried afterwards. That was worse in a way, although I felt pleased, in a way. He cried sitting at the kitchen table, like this, and asked me to forgive him, and told me to live my own life the way I wanted to. I remember him saying, "For God's sake, if you know how to go about it, be happy," blah

blah blah. He hit me a couple of times, a couple of times too many. He used to—well, all this was after Mum had come back and ruined his life anyway.'

'You never told me Clifford *hit* you.'

'Yes, well, he's my father.' Johnson stared into his cup. 'But I'm telling you now. And you know what else? I was going to tell you this the other day for some reason. He once told me he married Mum because she made him feel as if anything was possible, and he said it was only later that he thought perhaps she'd made him feel like that because she was unhinged.'

'Shall I tell you something I've never told you?'

'Sure.'

'You know my mother has no sense of humour?'

'If your mother had a sense of humour—' Johnson paused, probably to see whether he could devise a better way to wind me up than what had first sprung to mind, '—it would completely spoil her.'

'Thus speaks her most ardent fan,' I said. 'Honestly, what—you and I, but—anyway, so anyway, she did once tell me something that she prefaced by saying, "This is a complete joke, but—" which was a novel sort of formulation coming from her, right? But it was unforgettable anyway, like what you just said about your dad, because, well—'

'Ramble?'

'It's okay. I've never told anyone this before either.'

'I didn't say I'd never told anyone.'

'That's—' I thought about it, '—true. Okay, I myself, personally, me: I have never told anyone this before, what I'm about to tell you.'

Johnson, who had been tense before, grinned at me naughtily.

'It's not like that. When I told her I was getting married, she gave me two pieces of advice about how to get out of it again; I mean about how to get out of a marriage once you were in it, not about how to get out of getting into it in the first place. Am I making sense?'

'Keep trying.'

'I have to say I was fairly unimpressed at the time that that was her main idea of what to say on the subject.'

'I'm with your mother,' said Johnson, 'definitely.'

'Spare me, do. Anyway, so she says, "This is a complete joke, but I once ran away"—this is her speaking—"from Middleton." Surprised? Yes. She told me this herself. She said she ran away from him—by *bus*! Presumably he had the car that day or something. She wrote him a long letter all about how miserable he made her and everything about him she hated, and left it on the piano, and went to the bus station and got on the first bus out of town. Some hours later, she thinks to herself, maybe I've been a bit hasty. Next bus station they get to, she jumps out, buys a return ticket, and there she is, home in time to make supper. So the point is that when she got back, there's me, I suppose, and there's Middleton, and the letter is still on the piano. And the awful thing was that she hadn't stuck down the envelope properly, you know, she'd just put a speck of lick at the tip of the flap bit; so she removed the letter from the piano and for weeks—well, I don't know how long—she kept looking at the envelope trying to work out whether it had been opened and stuck shut again or not opened in the first place. And she just couldn't behave normally after that. You know why she sticks them like that? So she doesn't blot off her lipstick. Anyway, her advice was: "Don't send any letter until you're definite and certain that you want to be where you thought you were going when you got on the bus."'

'It's so great,' said Johnson, 'that she made this terrible mistake—possibly sent her marriage into its final tailspin—because of *lipstick*.'

'I knew you'd think that. Middleton ended it a few months later anyway.'

'I never thought I'd say this, but it's even better than her hoovering the lawn.'

'I have some shortbread,' I said. 'You want some?'

'Not after what I've eaten. You? Stay there. Is it in the cupboard? I'll get it.'

'In that tin,' I said, pointing.

My mother isn't mad the way Johnson's mother is mad. Johnson's mother is over the line—I don't know what the official diagnosis is; he doesn't like to talk about it. My mother is mad merely as in the lawn-hoovering incident. I wish Johnson hadn't been there that day because it confirmed, forever, everything about her that makes her delightful to him.

My mother had decided, for some reason of her own, that our pillows were too flat, and that it would be advantageous to cannibalise a couple of them for feathers for the rest. Although I'd never known her do anything like this before, the compulsion to interfere is entirely typical of her. What she wanted was a warm day with no wind so that she could work outside. Well, it was baking hot when she did the job and she managed to get feathers all over the place. As greater minds than hers have observed, it doesn't take much to disperse feathers. When she'd finished the job, she had a fit. She got two extension leads, plugged them together, took the hoover outside and hoovered the lawn. Johnson, aged about fifteen, watched her out of my bedroom window, ecstatic.

'So what was her other piece of advice?'

'What? Oh. It was: "Oh and by the way, if you *are* going to run away from your husband by bus, remember to do it at night."'

'Why?'

'I have no idea. I asked her, but—this is my mother we're talking about—her only explanation was that night time was good form: that if you run away from your husband by bus, you're better to do it at night.'

I have asked myself whether, if my mother had made a proper job of running away, Middleton would have brought me up. But I doubt it. He married again as soon as he could. I'm not sure my stepmother would have had me.

When I met her, Elise, for the first time, I had a fear equivalent to the newborn baby fear, except I wasn't 'oh so *very* much' waiting to fall in love: the reverse. There was a nebulous and disturbing period during which I waited to find out whether or not I would be able wholeheartedly to hate this unexpected adjunct to my family.

She and my father were already married. They took me out

to lunch. Never before in my life had I had so strong a sense that two grown-ups were trying to make a good impression on me.

'I don't know that that colour suits you,' said my father.

'I absolutely know what you mean,' Elise replied, fiddling with the trim on her dress. 'They promised me it was pistachio, but in daylight, good grief, this is the green of mosques and public lavatories.'

Because I deeply loved my father, I had imagined, without recognising it as a hope—I wasn't all that old—that he would have chosen a new wife just a little more like himself, or like me, I suppose. By the time I'd eaten my first course I was wondering what senseless impulse had caused him to select someone the same as my mother only worse. Of all things, if I can put it like this, my stepmother was, and will always be, the ex-manager of a soft-drinks factory. I've tried to get her to talk about it, I'd be very interested to know, but she won't discuss it with me.

Naturally, I later found out that she has her good side, but that's just boring. In the moment I discovered I didn't like her, I was filled with wayward relief.

Middleton told me once, in an uncharacteristically confessional speech, that his affection for my mother had slipped drastically the day he'd said, 'I find you very beautiful,' and she'd replied, 'But, what?—I'm not really?'

He said to me, 'You realise she doesn't hear herself the way she wants to unless someone else is listening?' This observation struck me as a viable approximation of the truth. 'We all want witnesses,' he said. 'Even hermits choose to assume that

God is lying on the cave floor next to them. A hermit, to a hermit, is obsessively on show.'

We didn't usually talk like this. When I grew up and left home, when my father came to visit me, we talked in the main about music. His music stories made him laugh, until he virtually cried, sometimes. He had a knack for making things funny that weren't funny at all, whatever that means. If you make something funny, I guess it's funny. He had a way of implying, *that's it*. He'd thump his knees. The right crazy remark would cause him to thump his knees, *that's it*, and then both of us would laugh with a kind of happiness that meant: funny?— are we laughing, or what?

A story of the type that induced a *that's it*, is the following. I don't remember whether it was about Stravinsky, Debussy, or Satie perhaps? I can't remember. 'Maestro,' says an earnest reporter, or academic, what have you, 'whither great music?' I'm not sure how the question was actually expressed. In effect, it's, *whither great music?* And the maestro replies, in this story, 'Great music will go wherever the next composer of genius wishes it to go.'

My father loved delivering this punchline. It put him right up there with those who are entitled to issue rebukes.

The best thing about Elise by a million miles turned out to be the fact that her first cousin was already in place as an informal stepmother to Johnson. This was while his real mother was away. Johnson's real mother spent time away. Then, later, she came back again and ruined Johnson's father's life. Before that, though, before Johnson's mother came home, my stepmother, Elise, went, for advice, to her cousin.

The upshot was that these two women threw me and Johnson together. Not only were the various households in question not that far apart, but Johnson's school and mine were at opposite ends of the same street. Almost at once we decided that if our stepmothers were cousins, we would be too, and that was that, and that is that, and for that I forgive everybody everything.

'Shall we shift ourselves?' He gestured towards the other room.

I was, as he had noticed, getting uncomfortable sitting in the kitchen. We stood up. Johnson looked prepared for something. We stood up but then didn't move.

'So what's the story?' he said.

'What's what story?'

'Don't give me that, Ramble. Tell me what's going on. Are you thinking of walking out on Con?'

'No. How would I do that? No, no. No, Con's already walked out on me—last Saturday.'

'You're kidding.'

I felt exhilarated, but the sigh that escaped me sounded pitiful.

'You aren't kidding,' he said. 'What's going on? Why? Wait a minute, I saw you on Sunday. Why didn't you say anything?'

'I was too embarrassed.'

'What's going on? Where is he? Why did he leave?'

'Oh, you know, I'm just—I'm completely useless and, last Saturday—!*bam!*—off he went. You know what he said? He said: "You're a vampire, you don't do anything, you just live inside your head. You don't give me any support with my music. You don't support me *full stop*. What's this crap about

cripples being *vulnerable*? You just"—Christ, he, he—"you just"
—he said: "Your work is rubbish, you hardly speak, and you
aren't even funny any more."'

Johnson had gone white. 'Jesus fucking Christ I'll fucking
kill him.'

'Oh yes *please* do,' I said, 'with piano wire, or you could
use the headphone leads, or at least cut his fingers off or—
hey—just saw his arms off at the elbow: zizzzz; and then—'

Johnson kissed me so hard I stumbled back against the
table and lost my balance; but he'd got me: he steadied me.
We kissed. I was amazed.

Suddenly he pulled back and laughed, as, helplessly, did I.

'Fuck it,' he said, 'that was nice.'

I found myself perched on—*nice*?—the table edge,
distressed that it was so swiftly over.

'Felt more like a statement than a question,' I said.
Immediately I had the feeling that this was a quote, the source
of which I'd forgotten.

'Switch your brain off, Ramble,' said Johnson. 'Let's just
call it incest and not get into anything complicated.'

'Oh right, fine,' I said.

'Listen,' he took hold of my arm, tight to make me concentrate, except that I was concentrating, 'listen, I have to say this
to you. For me—listen to me: in my universe, you *are* the
only girl in the world.'

'It was nice,' I said. 'And thank you. Thanks. Strange compli-
ments received with thanks.'

He muttered, too quietly for me to hear, and shook his
head, so that I missed reading the words off.

His eyes are usually grey, greyish, a warm grey, but are

sometimes almost green. They look their greenest when the whites are a bit bloodshot. I think this must be to do with complementary colours. Actually, I have no idea. Johnson's eyes, at their greenest, look very weird and interesting. They looked brightly weird now.

'Can I ask you something?' he said.

'Sure.'

'How do your hips affect having sex? I mean, presumably, do they?'

'My pelvis.'

'Pelvis, hips,' he said.

'My pelvis. Well, let's see, it's made me exceptionally careful about remembering to take the pill.'

'I didn't mean—'

'That's okay, sorry. I don't mind, I'll tell you. The hip, this hip, isn't really a problem. It can ache, but so what. The real problem is with my pelvic ligament. You want to hear? Basically—well you know this—I can't take skewed stress on it which is why I'm so bad on the stairs. Basically, if you stretch the ligament that bit too far, by whatever means, it's faint-makingly painful, and we're talking millimetres of difference. The pelvic ligament, if you read the literature, is classed as "pain-sensitive", to which I can only add, *I'll say*. Anyway, so—' I became slightly breathless which annoyed me, 'so what you're really asking me, re sex, since you ask, it's not so bad if you think about it because there's lots of ways a girl can do things without so much, as they say, spreading her legs, which is— that, for me, is exactly, but exactly the problem.'

A faint smile flittered over his face. 'If I *think* about it? You underestimate—'

'Guess what the cheapest Victorian streetwalkers were called, the slang term,' I said. 'Tuppenny Uprights.'

A penny for a newspaper full of lies and tuppence for a screw.

Johnson dismissed the excess information. He was, despite what he'd said, brooding on my limits. 'So ideally you'd be a mermaid,' he said.

'No.' I hesitated but couldn't help myself. 'Ideally, I'd be *normal*.'

'Hey,' he said, 'I'm on your side, all right?'

'I know, I'm sorry, it's just, I'm—speaking of being on one's side—' I wagged an eyebrow at him.

Johnson gave me a great big, open-hearted smile. The claustrophobic shabbiness of the flat was at once obliterated. I've always liked his face very much because it seems specially designed to look cheerful.

'So come to bed with me,' he said simply, 'and let's have whatever sort of fun we feel like when we get there.'

I stood up and then perched back on the table edge.

'Why, what? You don't fancy me?'

'Of course I do,' I said, feeling bizarre. It was bizarre to be saying something I never thought in my whole life I would say out loud.

'But, what?' he said.

'I don't know. You really want to? I am still married. I don't want to wake up and find I've turned into my mother.'

This objection by no means accurately expressed the feeling that had prompted me to say it.

'Don't be daft,' said Johnson. 'Apart from the fact that I worship her, as you well know—'

'Oh yes I know: she's knockout drops.'

'—I don't think she *loves* any of the men she sleeps with.'

I found myself gripping the table hard. At the same time I was suffused with a sort of secret, lazy vigour. *Love*? But of course. For a moment nothing meant anything to me at all.

'You're funny,' said Johnson. 'Anyway,' he stepped through to the other room, 'what about the sofa? You think it's wide enough? Look—' I stood up and followed him through, 'pillow for you,' he said, 'cushion for me, blanket for us both. It's all here. What more do we need?'

I was too pleased to speak. I closed the curtains, and as I did so, in about the same amount of time, he stripped himself.

'Johnson,' I said—well, I exclaimed it: 'Johnson! You're beautiful—I didn't realise, quite how, I don't know, look at you.'

'So?'

'What do you mean, *so*? What have you done to yourself? You're all—what do I say? Honed? Is that right?'

'Try *pumped*; except, you know, this—this is nothing.'

'Oh. I see. Well, I hadn't realised—I hadn't, I don't know— what you'd look like with no clothes on, that's all.'

Johnson laughed. 'You remind me of one of my boyfriends once, Zed, you remember you met him, little Zed? He used to—'

'Rhapsodise?'

'Yes, thank you.'

'I was thinking about him just recently. Of course I remember him. I liked him. I thought he was interesting.'

'Right, yes, sure; but all that kind of lyrical shit gets tiring in the end.'

'I'm somewhat partial to lyrical shit myself.'

'Tell me something I don't know. Should I get dressed again?'

'I think I need a drink,' I said. 'My mouth's gone dry. I guess all my juices have redirected themselves elsewhere.'

'Jesus Christ spare me,' said Johnson with comical horror. He sauntered back into the kitchen.

What a luxury, I thought—in a distant way: I'd never consciously thought about it before—what luxury to be able to make love to such a beautiful body.

The traffic in the street below sounded promising to me for the first time ever.

As he handed me the glass, Johnson said, 'Look, for reasons I don't want to go into, I have actually slept with a couple of girls before, just to be clear about it.'

'You have? Really?'

'Yes.'

'Really?'

'Not both at once, I don't mean.'

'But that's worse.' I drank the water down. 'You've done it twice. That makes me feel cross.'

'Good, I'm glad to hear it. Ramble, why don't you give me that,' he took the empty glass back, 'and get your clothes off.'

'I have to say one more thing.'

'What?'

'Well I didn't explain properly myself. It's not that I can't do whatever I like, more or less, or whatever you like, I don't know what you think you—basically, I more or less can do whatever; it's just that, some ways I pay for it afterwards, that's all, but that's okay, there's a beneficial element of anaesthetic that comes into play when—it's not even anaesthetic, a sort of override, but—'

'Please, no,' he said, distressed, 'don't talk like that.'

'Well okay, I was just—I don't want you to—you're—' I lost my thread. I'm so wretchedly skimpy, I thought, meagre, spindly-limbed. I have bruises on me. The elastic seams on the brace leave welts. I'm wretchedly meagre, spindly, skimpy—

'Ramble—'

I spoke over him. 'You know what Con said about you? He called you a "tasteless faggot".'

Johnson slowed down in some fundamental, dangerous fashion. For a frightening instant I thought he was going to leave, even though that was why I'd mentioned it.

'Anything else you want to share with me?'

'No.'

Johnson controlled himself. He didn't leave, he just said, 'Fine,' and then added, 'Look, Ramble, watch your fucking mouth, you idiot. Fuck the bloody lot of it.' When I didn't move, he said, 'Come on. Behave yourself. Stop pissing around.'

And then he began to undress me. I was still feeling frightened, but I knew he didn't want me to feel frightened. I was telling myself: don't be—why be frightened?—he's still here.

'Anyway, so what, I've seen you naked before,' he said.

'What?'

'That time you did twisty poles into Kathleen Graham's swimming pool.'

Kathleen Graham? I would have been about thirteen.

He finally got my top off, I wasn't being particularly helpful, but he stopped then and said, 'I have a confession to make, since we've been saying all these things.'

'Yes?'

'You know when I knew about myself for totally certain? When half my classmates at school started asking me why I wasn't trying to have it off with you. "What's the matter with you, man? What's your problem?—If you don't want her, I'll have her.—Hey Pike, you fairy, you're not a *fairy* are you?— What's going on? Cousins is okay. Cousins is allowed.—Have you seen the way she—"' Johnson broke off. He coloured.

'What?' I asked. 'The way she what?'

Almost whispering, he said, '"Have you seen the way she moves?"'

I think I coloured, myself.

'Don't go away inside your head,' he said.

I put the back of my hand to his cheek in forgiveness.

Johnson walked round behind me to undo my not entirely necessary bra. He was entertainingly inept with the bra.

'Please tell me honestly,' I was facing the sofa, found myself addressing the book shelves, 'I don't want you to feel, if this is, I don't know, uncomfortable to your instincts—I don't want you to feel—'

'Delicately put, but I'm a slut really, don't worry about it.'

'Well that's not delicately put.'

'I think you'll find it's true though.'

As he unzipped my skirt, and pulled apart my brace, I turned and tilted towards him, ranged my arms around him and kissed him in the hollow of his neck. The taste of his skin unhinged me slightly, it had the same kind of heft to it as the smell of laundry scorching on a radiator. The very first day we met, sitting on the metal bench in my father's then new garden, I'd been overcome with a wish to kiss Johnson's neck. He'd been wearing a pale blue, short-sleeved cotton shirt with the top two buttons undone and—

'You're quaint,' he whispered. I could feel the rush of his voice on my cheek and a small commotion of laughter.

'Quaint?'

'Come on,' he said.

Somehow we lay down on the sofa.

'Is it possible,' said Johnson, holding me tight, murmuring to me, 'that you could completely stop thinking now? I mean I really mean it this time.'

The curtains billowed. The Minimart bell pwanged. The fridge thermostat clicked to off: its tedious hum ceased. The air smelled warm, Johnson smelled warm. He was taut and beautiful, alive. I wasn't sure I was allowed to reply, so I bit him.

7

Friday

I heard the alarm clock go off upstairs. Johnson didn't stir.

I remembered Mrs Marechal saying that Stella Ramble's old people's home was a great hospital, but not a great hotel. This sofa, I thought, is a big sofa but not a big bed. As a result, Johnson and I were still tangled up together. And it was a joy, no matter what the cost, to find myself this way, still entangled in the morning. I drifted off for a while without thought, sleeplessly asleep.

When Johnson did wake up, I re-awoke. He got dressed in a hurry. As far as I was able to, so did I. The room was surprisingly cool.

'I'll do it.' Johnson put his fancy musculature to use and fixed the brace around me tighter than I could ever do it myself. 'Ramble, your stomach's making sounds like a whole zoo full of freaky birds.'

'It's called an aviary.'

'I do know that.'

'I know, I'm sorry. I haven't been eating terribly well.'

'Shall I go down and buy you a croissant or something?'

'No, I can go later. It's okay.'

'Don't *not* look after yourself, all right? You're my number one girl.'

'I believe you.'

He drew the curtains. The light was brilliant, but whitish for the first time in days.

'It's no trouble,' he said, staring down into the street. 'Is there anything you'd like? Can I make you some toast?'

'Stargazy pie.'

'What?'

'Stargazy pie: Cornish fish pie.' He didn't react. 'It's a Cornish fish pie where all the fish heads are arranged so that they stick up out of it at the sides.'

'Don't talk daft, Ramble.' He went to the door and put on his grass-green coat. He was putting his coat on, not just his clothes. I hadn't realised he'd be leaving so quickly. Didn't he want something himself, bread and butter, a coffee? I didn't want to be left on my own. My heart started to beat a little faster. 'It's not daftness,' I said, but I could see he didn't believe me. Anyway, I *was* being daft. I didn't want fish pie for breakfast.

'Ramble, I meant to ask you last night, have you said anything to your mother?'

'Please.'

'I didn't want to land you in it.'

'My mother? Have I said anything to my mother?'

Johnson put his fist to his mouth and spoke in a tannoy voice. 'Ground Control calling Ramble. Ground Control calling Ramble. Friendly life form detected at three o'clock. Proceed to interact with friendly life form.'

'See here, as the Americans say, next time you get in trouble, *you* talk to my mother.'

'Oh, believe me,' he said.

'Really? You talk to my mother?'

'You sound so superior. She always says I'm right whatever I do and as I screw up on a regular basis, it's, you know, relaxing.'

'Very, I'm sure. Are you really telling me you call my mother?'

'You can tease me about liking her, but I do. What do you want me to say? I also like fireworks, prawn cocktails and watching England play cricket.'

'You know she keeps her mobile in her bra?'

'Fantastic!' he shouted, and then said, 'Well, so long, I'm out of here.' He opened the door and stepped backwards onto the landing.

I felt unhappy. I went to say goodbye. Fleetingly, like the gentleman hero of a black-and-white movie, he kissed me on the cheek.

'Johnson—'

The sense between us stretched.

'Anyway, babe,' he said, 'you'd better not ask me again.'

I had to look at his face to see what he meant. 'Oh. Did I ask?'

He palpably considered replying, but chose instead to smile.

'Anyway yourself,' I said, moving a step away from him, 'it's going to take me a bit to recover, let alone—God knows.'

'But you're all right? Your hip, your *pelvis*?' He leant forwards looking anxious and put a hand to me.

'You know, it is a possibility I could get better. I could

improve. It happens, but it also sometimes doesn't. I don't know, there's the option of screwing a metal plate across both sides. It's called plating. It's supposed to make the thing rigid but it doesn't always work. I don't want to do that; but I'll definitely get a new hip when I'm older. That's going to be ace, definitely. There's nothing wrong with me.'

'You'll do,' said Johnson. He smiled—until I couldn't help somewhat smiling back—then leant round to my better ear and whispered, '*Twisty poles.*'

That was it: he gadded off down the stairs, doing up his enormous coat buttons one-handed and whistling some riff I didn't recognise. He could hardly have seemed more insouciant had he simultaneously been dandling a roll-up and balancing an open carton of coffee.

I reminded myself what a complete twit Johnson can be, and wondered whether there would ever come a day when we would speak to any extent about what we'd done.

But I suspect not, I rather think not, because afterwards—afterwards but before we fell asleep—on the dirty old sofa and folded in my arms, convulsively, as I'd held him, he'd wept.

Out of sight he paused and called up, 'Hey Ramble, I'm being spirited away for the weekend by a dishy architect. Loads of money, very good manners, horse racing statto of all things; don't know where he's taking me. Shall I call you on Monday and tell all? Deal?'

'Deal!' I shouted, and imagined the word, 'deal', plunging down the stairwell.

'Maximagantic!' cried Johnson from below.

'What?'

Friday

He rattled down the bottom flight of stairs laughing and yelling, 'He calls me Ben!'

'Samuel,' I mumbled, but then I felt probably I was wrong. Ben Jonson, *The Alchemist*, &c., doesn't have an 'h', but I thought: no no, he means the athlete—beautiful body, the best in its day, except, pumped on drugs. Well, I thought, who cares what he means?

Johnson hadn't noticed, tumbling out of my eyrie, that he'd trodden on a folded piece of paper placed just outside the flat door on the landing. I bent over, slightly yelped with pain, picked it up and read: 'Well its time to say by thnks be smart youre alright see ya Chantal Jarvis.'

I was listening for Johnson to shout up something else, but heard only the click as he opened the front door and the bang as he closed it.

I'm not sure why, but I trudged up to the bedroom with the blanket and pillow and, once there, re-read my finished and dispatched ice article. It was one of the worst pieces I've ever done. I weighed up the likelihood of anyone noticing and asking me to improve it. I almost hoped they would, on the grounds that it might be pleasant to work for editors who were rational judges of my work. The reason I didn't *actually* hope they would was that I simply couldn't think how I'd be able to face giving even a single minute more of my time to a project so utterly worthless.

I thought about Mrs Shaw—*Chantal Jarvis*?—telling me to dose up more. I was not 'alright'. So fine then, I thought, fine, I'll pop a DF118. I'll do it. It's not like I'm going anywhere.

My doctor gave me sixty pills in the spring, I don't often take them, and I was thinking that I still had over forty, except that when I looked, I found I didn't have any. The DFs were missing. For no particular reason, I'd kept my supply in my underwear drawer. I was interested, and vaguely amused, but also hurt to discover that my worst-case pills were gone. *After all that*, I thought, and had the thousand-flap, railway-departures-board sensation in my mind.

I went reluctantly to the bathroom. Coproxamol, not as strong, ought to be in the medicine cabinet. I hesitated, but those pills, anyway, were still there. Yes: two, four times a day. 'Do not exceed the recommended—' &c. Given that I was taking anything at all, I wanted to be taking DFs, codeine type stuff, whatever. I swallowed three coproxamol and sat on the lid of the loo, at which I thought: why sit on the loo, at least go downstairs and sit on the sofa. As I was thinking, *at least go downstairs and sit on the sofa*, someone rapped at the flat door.

I got to my feet. Don't hurry, I said to myself. But who was it? I hurried, thinking: *three* coproxamol?—stupid, stupid.

'Me again,' said Mr Harbottle with sly jollity.

I stared at the floor.

'You know what's happened to the people downstairs?'

'What?' I asked him.

'No, cheeky. I'm asking you,' he said.

'But what has happened? I don't know.' Indignation made me feel as though I was speaking the truth.

'They've buggered off is what,' he said, 'bloody looters the pair of them, buggered off with half the fixtures and fittings. Call me an idiot, I knew they were fly, but I didn't think they'd—' He interrupted himself. 'Is your rent in the post?'

I thought, half *what* fixtures and fittings? I tried to appear normal by lifting my gaze somewhat nearer to his. 'I don't know. I'll have to ask my husband.'

The man with a prick like a lever handle looked me up and down.

'Listen missus,' he said, 'do not lie to the King of Bullshit. Harbottle is inheritor of an ancient lineage of Northumbrian bullshitters, so don't try it on with me. When one of us kicks the bucket, it's not dirt goes on our coffins, we shovel one hundred per cent proof genuine first-class pure Andalusian bullshit, you hear me? You get plants growing on them graves you only grow in greenhouses. Don't bullshit a Harbottle, you hear? What you got in your purse anyway?'

Andalusian bullshit! I didn't at first take in that he'd asked a question. 'Ten quid?' I said.

'Give us that then and knock it off the rent. And I want *that* by Monday, you understand me?'

As I got my purse out of my bag he talked militantly into the air. 'You saying you didn't suss her out? Because I tell you here and now, she had her little game same as he did. She's a right one. No better than she should be? *Don't even.* I don't like people pissing me around. I don't like it *a lot* I don't. I tell her, okey dokey, you've got yourself three days' grace. And what does she do? She scarpers.'

I gave him what he'd asked for and stood in the doorway, helpless, as Mr Harbottle glanced at my money, turned and went downstairs, singing a funny song. I heard it go round the corners. *'I love me daughter, More than I oughter, I had a meal of lemon peel, But now I feel that melons could be*—Hello, hello,' he said.

'How do.'

'Little lady doesn't seem too sure about the rent.'

'No problem,' came the light reply.

'Monday then,' said Mr Harbottle.

I stepped backwards, stumbled several paces backwards, hit the near arm of the sofa and fell like a heap of sticks and heard myself gasping and knew that this was pain, though I had the brace on, extraordinarily tight, I felt it hold me and—as I fell, I fell into a haze.

Somehow I knew I needed to haul myself up again, fast. How, I'm not sure, but I did it—got myself up, sitting, organised on the sofa. *Why are legs funny?* There I sat, like Stella Ramble, who has nothing to do, repetitively smoothing my skirt out over my knees.

I grew up an English child. I have been civilised with bad jokes so I sat there waiting, hazy but aloof, and measured my racing heartbeat against Con's slow footfall on the stairs.

He pushed the open door, dropped a bag down, slouched in, kissed me on the top of my head, went into the kitchen, filled a glass with water, came back, sat down next to me, and there we were, side by side facing forwards.

I thought: perhaps he's here as a kindness, to see me square with the rent, and to pick up a few of his things. Perhaps he'll go away again at once in a few minutes, or seconds.

'Hello,' he said.

'*How do.*'

He sighed. He took a drink of water. 'So how's things? Okay? Where are we, Friday? I've been working so hard I'm

210

a bit out of it. Did you meet your deadline on that ice thing?'

My answer came out politely all by itself. 'I haven't sent it yet. I have to check a couple of details. Then I can send it off.'

'Well, great. You're basically there. That's great. Good.' He drank some more. 'So did you decide to include the Moscow of the Orient?'

'I'd already started that bit before you left.'

'Good, well, don't bite my head off.'

I was still hearing him coming up the stairs. 'Do you really have the rent?' I asked.

He laughed. 'You don't know about this, okay?' He held open his jacket with mock furtiveness and flashed what looked to be a great wad of tenners in the inside pocket.

The blackbird was singing outside.

'So you've been pretty busy?' he said. He could have been a bad visitor in an old people's home. TEETH PULLED WHILE YOU WAIT.

My hands had the shakes, severely, like someone short of a fix; but it felt as though if I controlled my hands I would cry instead, so I let them shake. I heard myself reply—I thought: *oh dear*—'Sufficient unto the day the weather thereof.'

'Don't bust my balls, okay? I'm sorry, okay?' Con slumped back, sighing some more, resting the glass of water on his stomach. 'One thing I would ask of you is just don't ask me where I've been. I should've—not have left you like that, I know, but it's too late to change that, so just let's drop it, okay. Mostly I've been working at Joe's, but I won't pretend that's all. I don't want to be dishonest with you. But as far as the rest, it's just going to be simpler if we forget it, okay, for you, I mean, not just me. I swear on my life there isn't anyone else. I didn't go off with someone else, not like that. It wasn't that, Ramble, I promise you, I swear, okay? I know I said a lot of shit things to you and it probably wasn't very helpful. Coming clean brings up a lot of dirt obviously, right? That was supposed to be witty. Okay, forget it. What I want to say to you is this. You've got to trust me. There's nothing much to say anyway. I can't explain right now. I've had a weird time, seriously fucking weird. But it was a one-off. There's no need to look sardonic. You don't want to go to marriage guidance?'

'No.'

'I didn't think so.' He finished the water. 'The thing is, I've missed you, against the odds you might think. Don't take that the wrong way. I think you need help, I seriously do. You need to see someone. I've been thinking about this. It's been rough times for us—since the beginning essentially, especially for you of course, I'm not pretending it's been so hard for me. But, I don't know why, by the end of last week I'd got right to the end of my rope, I'd just completely fucking had it. I needed to clear my head and I had to get away so—so as to do so. It's been intense, but what I'm saying is, let's just forget all this, carry on as we were but have it in mind that we could make things better. How about it? I seriously think you need to find someone you can talk to.'

'Listen,' said Con, 'the thing is, am I allowed to say this? I've been under a lot of stress recently. My whole career just isn't— it isn't going the way I want it to. It isn't just months going past, it's turning into years. I've been having this shitty feeling that I need more time. I keep thinking I need to reorganise my life somehow. I've been getting more and more stressed out, basically, and I know I should have talked to you about it, but somehow, I don't know. But I should have, obviously. I mean obviously. I mean, it's good to talk.'

Here he ground to a halt.

I said, 'That's the advertising slogan for British Telecom.'

'Jesus, Ramble, give me a fucking break. I'm trying to apologise to you. Haven't you got any thoughts about any of this? These things are never all one way, you know. I'm not just making it all up.' He took a shuddering breath. 'So how have you been?'

'Okay.'

'What have you been up to?'

'Nothing,' I said. 'The usual: library, Stella Ramble, work, the usual.'

'Good for you,' he said. 'Listen, Ramble, let's forget about all this, let's put what's happened behind us and try and make a go of things, that's what I'm saying. Really. You know, consider yourself lucky by the way. All I did was take a few days off. The bloke downstairs told me last week he knocked his wife out with a saucepan. Ramble, please look at me sometimes when I'm talking to you.'

'He told you he knocked her out with a saucepan?'

'Yes—why?'

'They've done a flit,' I said.

'Seriously? Are you serious?'

I was over the terrible, immediate shock of my fall, but I couldn't keep my hands still.

'—asleep at the wheel,' said Con. 'I *said*,' he continued, 'how have you been? You're not telling me much. You know,' he laughed dejectedly, 'for someone who thinks they like words, it's not as if you're any good with them.'

Once again he halted.

He was waiting for an answer. I reached for anything to say. How had I been? I didn't know. I could barely hear the noises inside my head. 'Guess what?'

'What?' said Con.

What? What? 'One night I thought I saw a buzzard fly up the street.'

He made two fists but opened his fingers again quickly. 'Okay, tell me about that if you like.'

I pictured it. I closed my eyes. I flew the bird through my mind. Could this shape possibly have been a buzzard? The idea was so improbable. He'd asked me to say something. I had nothing to say. 'It went from left to right.'

'You know, you can sit there being peculiar,' he said. 'Well, it took a lot out of me to come back, you know. Just don't make it worse straight away. Bad move. Let me say something. You're so off-hand about music. When I asked you to marry me I thought music would be the thing that secretly bound us together. Well, not secretly. Why did I say *secretly*? I don't mean to accuse you or anything, but you misled me on that one. I want to write good music, Ramble—I'd, I'd like to write great music, surprisingly enough. You know, it's possible to do that even if you are personally lacking. Carlo Gesualdo, Prince of Venosa, was pretty much of a nutcase but he came out with the most wonderfully advanced harmonies. Phenomenal. Nobody else wrote harmonies like him for centuries afterwards. And as far as being a lowlife human being, beat this. He was a murderer. What I didn't expect was that you were going to be,' Con's voice rose, 'so disengaged about music. I kept thinking, why couldn't I get through to you? I don't need you to know what a hemiola is or whatever, but I thought you'd be able to hear something like that, or if you hear it but you're just not admitting, which I strongly suspect, I had thought I'd be able to talk to you about that sort of thing, about how music works, why we wait passionately for a certain chord in a certain piece, why it can make you want to cry, what's going on, you know? But you're—I mean, it's fine, but all of this, our marriage, it's taken me a lot of getting used to because I thought I was getting into something very different. You're one of the most, the most insular fucking people I know. You don't think you are, but I've tried being up front with you and it's like throwing stones down a well. That's why I started using head-phones all the time, in the end.'

'I mind about that.'

'Of course you do,' he said. 'Of course you do. That's why I did it. I wanted you to mind. Look, do you just want to go to bed?'

My voice came out in a whisper. 'Not just now, I don't think, if that's all right?' I glanced round at him, dreading that he might insist, but he said, 'No, that was—no—stupid, I'm sorry. I should have waited for you to suggest it.'

'Archie—' I said.

'I know, I spoke to him.'

I locked my hands between my knees. 'What have you been up to yourself,' I asked, 'that you can tell me I just mean, I'm not prying; that you don't mind saying about?'

'God, you can't imagine it's been such a nightmare, I had to churn out God knows how many minutes a day, and coffee

and glucose powder just isn't enough after a while so—fuck—
I've been rubbing coke on my gums for three days straight
and I've had enough. Which isn't to say, I mean, Anthony
said my work on the Prague cues ended up some of the best
stuff I've ever done. Even Uncle Joe said it was good stuff—
despite, n.b., *incredibly* boring film. I've been at Uncle Joe's
most of the time, Ramble. There was a real to-do on so I slept
over there. I've been there most of this week, and I slept there
last night after the session because I was totally busted, or
"spunked out" as Joe says. They let me off going to the sessions
today, Bill's helping: Air. Hello? Air Studios. I assumed you'd
figured out where I was?'

'Let's just pretend none of this happened,' he repeated.
  'None of what happened?'
  'Exactly! There you go,' he said.
  'You want to carry on as before, end of story?'
  'What story?' He sounded both weary and almost smug. 'I
didn't tell anyone I left, did you? I'm betting not. Did you? I
knew it. So, hey, nothing's happened, end of story. Honestly
Ramble, let's just forget it. I don't want us to be stuck with
some sort of feeling like this is the aftermath of something, okay?
What? You're going to tell me "aftermath" meant something
fucked in 1724? You're listening to the blackbird in the lime
tree? You know, it's very nearly singing "Rudolph the Red-Nosed
Reindeer". Ramble, please, I know I may have hurt you—well,
may, I dare say, no doubt, but, but in a way, it could be—it's
good to get some of these problems, you know, out in the open.'
  'You just told me to pretend nothing had happened.'
  He made an infuriated noise.

'You'd like me to learn my lesson but not talk about it?' I said.

'Please don't get sarcastic on me right now. I'm really really tired, you have no idea. I'm clobbered. Anyway, tell me, have you done something to your hair?'

'What? No. Why?'

He pointed at the can of hairspray on the book shelves. 'Lucky I didn't chance it and say how nice you were looking.' As his own words sank in with him, he gave a little cough of a laugh. 'Sorry, that didn't come out right. I did sleep a bit last night. You wouldn't know it.' He cleared his throat and added, 'So what's with the hairspray?'

'It's not important. It was a mistake. Venosa, did you say?'

'Yes, Carlo Gesualdo, Prince of Venosa.'

'Where's that?'

'It's near—' He couldn't remember. 'He was massively ahead of his time, plus, well, he murdered his wife.'

'There's something I need to tell you,' I said.

I wanted to explain about music, but I couldn't express myself clearly.

'When I say—when I tell someone my father's last words were, "I'll see myself out," I'm hoping that's what they were, to make it sound graceful, supposing he died on purpose—supposing it all really ended at the end, so to speak. But the truth is I have no idea what he said. Afterwards, you know, my mother told me he'd said something like, "Don't come down"; but when I pressed her, she wasn't sure. It's just a wish on my part, it isn't something I know, when I say he said, "I'll see myself out."'

'No big deal,' said Con. 'Don't worry about it. I also spoke to your mother. I asked her exactly the same thing not long after, what was the last thing he said, and when she told me about it she said he said something like, "I'll hop it now. You stay put."'

I felt a taste of danger in my mouth, as though I was suddenly primed for violence.

'This isn't a cheap shot,' said Con, he continued talking, 'but one of the reasons I'm in thrall to music, to what music can do, as against words—besides perhaps having some kind of physiological predisposition to be affected by it—a serious reason why I'm different from you is that, unlike words, there can never be anything dishonest about trying to make music do what it does as perfectly as possible.'

I don't think it occurred to him that I might have a reply to this. At any rate, he didn't pause for a reply. 'Oh yes,' he said, 'there's something else. I want you to listen to something.'

Instead of getting up to play a few bars on the keyboard, Gesualdo's advanced harmonies, or one of the Prague cues perhaps, he put his empty water glass down on the floor and stayed where he was, fishing around in his side pockets.

I had a funny idea of him giving me a zircon ring, but what he was looking for turned out to be a cardboard box about the size of a pack of cards. He opened it himself, drew out a miniature, cellophane-wrapped mechanism, then gently cursed and fiddled with it until it emitted a deranged buzzing noise, like the death throes of an oxygen-deprived bluebottle.

'There,' said Con. 'How do you like that? Pretty damn neat and pretty damn quiet. If that doesn't wake me I'll be trusting you to do the job instead.'

He stood up and started to wander round the room. 'So here's how it's going to be,' he said. 'You are listening, right?

You know, please listen to me. I've been thinking about this a lot. So I'll stop composing through headphones, okay? And I'll tell you about the cues, okay? And we'll talk about, I don't know, books, whatever. Whatever you like. Whatever. I want us to try harder. When I left last weekend, obviously, I mean obviously, I put us further apart, but I missed you just the same as I pretty well miss you even when we're together. Okay? Please? I've come back and I want us to try a bit harder.' He bent down and kissed me on the top of my head again and murmured, 'Don't punish me, okay? If you think about it you might agree with me that you—can be, you can be unkind. But I'm saying let's just look forwards and try to forget all the stupid details.'

'—call Mr Harbottle,' Con paced back and forth, back and forth, 'or speak to him on Monday and ask if we can move downstairs when the damp's been fixed. I don't know why we didn't think of this before, but it would mean I could have an upright, I want a Yamaha, second-hand I mean, or fourth-hand and bashed to bits probably—but the best one I can afford, one with a mute pedal.' He let his hand stray to the pocket that had all the ten-pound notes stuffed into it. 'I don't want to disturb anybody. I think that would solve everything. I'll keep the electric keyboard for if I have to work all night, but I'll basically play the upright and you can hear what you like and I'll talk through the cues with you if you like, that would be great. The touch on this keyboard continually fucks me off. I would so love to be able to have a proper piano again. Obviously the hallway and stairs means the downstairs flat's smaller, but perhaps we could off-load some of your books. It's not as if you read them all the time, and it would mean you wouldn't have to go up all these stairs, because, obviously, they've made you worse. I mean, that's right, right? We don't talk about these things enough. What do you think? I know we only meant to stay here temporarily, and it's been, what, nearly three years, but I'm thinking, this way we can start again. What do you think? After all, this area is improving.'

'But who would live up here?' I said.

'What does that matter?'

The blackbird was still at it. 'You know,' I said, 'the lime leaves haven't even *started* to fall yet.'

'Is that supposed to be poetic?'

'No, I was just mentioning.'

'I might have a bath,' he said. 'I actually did have a shower when I got up, but I still feel really skanky. It's more my brain than anything. My brain needs a bath. You know how my dad says, "Don't overdo it." This entire week's pretty much I've been overdoing it. I mean, no that doesn't come close—I mean, Ramble, I've been right at my limit.'

He flumped back down next to me on the sofa. 'Ramble, please just forget last weekend. I didn't mean what I said. I was angry about everything. It's not your fault. We'll carry on as before just fine. Please, okay. I mean, whatever I said bad, you forgive me and I'll forgive you. I'm so tired. I'm going to have to sleep first before I do anything else. I fold.' He keeled over sideways, closed his eyes and drew his legs up so that the soles of his shoes rested against the side of my leg.

His eyes were shut.

I twisted round and gripped the back of the sofa, bit the inside of my lip to stop myself yelping again, then raised my stiffened body up and pushed hard away. Mercifully, I rocked far enough in one go to get balanced on my feet. There's a level of physical pain, distressing enough, where you can still decide to force your way through it. That was what I decided I would do.

'This sofa's so great,' said Con, stretching himself out, his head on the velvet cushion, 'considering it's stuck together with Velcro.'

I thought: and me—also stuck together with Velcro? I noticed, I was disconcerted, that the shoes he was wearing were new. He was more gaunt than usual. He did look unbelievably tired. He was in the scruffy suit he'd been wearing when he left, but had on a new, bright white tee shirt.

'Con?'

'Yes?' He couldn't resist employing a tone that suggested he knew I was about to say something perverse.

'I'm going for a walk.'

'What?'

'I'm going for a walk.'

'A walk?'

'Yes.'

'Really? I mean, fine, okay, if I must. I can see taking a walk, if that's what you want.'

'No, no, don't, please, it's fine. I want some fresh air and—' Only at this juncture did I remember that I had instinctively lied to him about the ice piece. 'I've got to go to the library to check one last thing for my article. I need to do that and send it off. It's, you know—'

'Am I somehow not fresh air?' he said. 'No, all right. Sorry. You go for a walk. I mean I can come if you like. Or would you not like me to?'

Or would you not like me to? It struck me that the reply 'yes' and the reply 'no' would both mean: *no*. I felt grateful for this quirk in the language.

'For fuck's sake, are you going or not?' Con opened his eyes. Still as I was, I froze. 'Make sure you put your coat on,' he said, closing them again, 'it's chilly outside.'

I waited for more.

When there was no more, I turned and hobbled silently away. I slipped my coat on, slung my bag on, and started for the chilly outside.

I had to take the stairs step by step with pauses. I'd left my crutches behind so that he wouldn't find them missing: not rational. I was both shocked and surprised that he'd come back, even though I'd fearfully half expected it all along. *It's too much. I've had it up to here. Leave me alone. No no no.*

I should have taken the stairs sitting, but the violent part of me baulked at this idea. My thoughts were a mess, they fell over, jammed, fell over, jammed, fell too fast to—jammed—make sense, *so how's things?*—fell—what?—dirty carpet tiles, the sofa, the Minimart, Whitby harbour, the Lady of Shalott, zircon, Goldilocks, Mecanorma Graphoplex, the Elgin Marbles, Madame Tussaud's, the pigeons, Andalusian bullshit, an autistic vampire, CAT CHEWS FACE OFF NUN.

Listen, Ramble, let's forget about all this. Oh yes? He walked out, he's walked in again, he'd like to leave a little gap in the story. It isn't true he's been at Uncle Joe's most of the week. It's Friday. Anthony phoned up sometime on Tuesday. That doesn't leave most of the week.

You're better off keeping well out. She's called—*Chantal Jarvis?*

Friday

Well, I don't know, do I care what he was doing? *It's been a while now since I've thought of myself as your husband.* What do I care? It was supposed to be the end: he said so. Now we're back in the *middle*? End, middle. *I wanted you to mind.*

If this is part of the middle, I thought, I don't specially care about anything. Who cares about the middle? All you can say about the middle is, the more difficult it becomes, the more like real life it is. In short, the worse, the better—though—subtly, all the same, the worse. Why would anyone care about a gap in the middle? *He was massively ahead of his time, plus, well, he murdered his wife.*

> A WIFE'S RIGHTS: "Wife," said a married man, looking for his bootjack, after she was in bed, "I have a place for all things, and you ought to know it by this time." "Yes," replied she, "I ought to know where you keep your late hours, but I don't."

So what, *gaps*, I said to myself. Suppose an asteroid were to wipe out almost all of what we presently think of as civilisation, what good would it do the epigraphers of the future to trip over a twisted metal instruction panel off the front of a Japanese used-knicker coin-op vending machine? *Consider yourself lucky.* Oh yes? *Despair, Irresolution, Diffidence, Languor, Fits, Piles, Worms, &c.* Browning:

> I thought,—All labour, yet no less
> Bear up beneath their unsuccess.

I thought,—I was only part way down the stairs. I leant into a still-dusty corner for respite and wondered to myself—*this*

223

isn't a cheap shot: if a person were to write a music cue for the conversation Con and I just had on the sofa, what would constitute playing *with* the scene? *Just let it drop, okay.* He hates background music, because, if there's music he wants to listen to it. Nevertheless, his job is to work on background music of which most listeners will barely be conscious. Suppose he were now commissioned to write his own cue for our scene on the sofa—*n.b., incredibly boring film*—surely he would make the offensive character reeling off garbage about carrying on as before seem really rather sad, *tender* even?

Make your own fucking friends. How? I warm to people who read books. I like the way they sit, hunched over, deliberately deaf—a reader is an autistic vampire, like me.

I passed Mrs Shaw's door, what had been her door. I found I did care about her story, gaps, details. I ran the previous Saturday through my head one more time.

Con leaves our flat, whips down the first flight of stairs and encounters Mr Shaw.

Con says, 'I've done it. I said I would. I've left my wife. I'm out of here.'

Mr Shaw, who had been on his way up hoping to cadge a few quid off his new mate, turns, and they go down together.

'Nice,' says Mr Shaw, trousering Con's money. 'Me, I bloody knocked mine out with a fucking saucepan.'

They laugh, two doors slam, and that's it.

I thought, *Forget all the stupid details? The stupid details? Forget* them? I tried to count and gave up somewhere around 900,000. I could have got to a million, I'm fairly certain, a million if I'd tried hard enough. *You are listening?* I leant briefly against the front door, leant against it with my forehead.

What's the stupidest detail of all? I asked myself, and straight away I knew. It was that, once I'd lost the ability to walk properly, right when I first left home, the odd occasions when my father came to visit me in the places where I subsequently lived, he always left with the words, 'I'll see myself out.'

Out in the open, on the street, I felt better, though I was conscious of being woozy still, a little de-tuned. I thought to myself that it was perhaps partly the pills, and wondered whether taking three of them had contributed to my falling over. The diesel-heavy air was cold and pleasant. There was no smell of residual heat. Presumably it had cooled all night. What was I doing? I wouldn't have minded whiling away an hour or so in one of the white plastic chairs outside the minicab office.

To my slight regret the ten-pound-note man was nowhere in view, but I did see the *Big Issue* man sitting on an empty sports bag near the entrance—his pitch—to the Minimart.

I set off.

'Long time, dot dot,' I said. 'How's things?'

'Long time *no see*. Not too bad. Yourself?' he said.

I shrugged.

'Want one?' he asked.

'Ah well, ah,' I replied, 'this week is definitely one of those weeks.'

When it's *one of those weeks* I just hand over a pound. He's not supposed to take it but we don't care. He gets a dab more change than otherwise, I save forty pence, he has an extra

Issue to sell, I don't have to read it, not that I mind reading it, and we both end up feeling comradely.

'Knock knock,' he said.

I replied, with less than requisite good humour, 'Who's there?'

'Big Ish—'

'Big Ish—*who*?'

'One pound forty please.'

'Take the pound, buddy,' I said, and winked at him, which is not something I do at all often to anybody.

A young man walked past us and spat at our feet.

When he was out of earshot, I said, 'Isn't it a pleasure to be able to hate a person with no prospect of ever having to revise your opinion.'

I knew this remark would annoy the *Big Issue* man and it did. He looked away from me and launched into a high-flown account, as far as I could understand him, of compassion, not of spitting, mind you. There's a speedy way he talks, rehearsed clauses I tend to assume, that I find hard to follow, so I stood there and flirted with a sense of getting too cold, until it came to me that my annoying the *Big Issue* man on purpose was an act of charity one might measure against that of a piano tuner allowing himself to be insulted by an ugly waitress. I felt almost inspired.

The Minimart doors slid apart and out came the woman who'd worn the clingy tiger-print top on Ice Cream Sunday, who worries twentyfour-seven about her children. She had three heavy bags of shopping, plus her son, I take it, who followed behind her in his pricey footwear. He was saying, 'Not an *Easter* egg. A hot *air* balloon.' Billy—was it?—who wakes his mother up early. I liked his remark. She didn't seem to have heard him; but then, neither, presumably, did I.

How can it be, I thought, shifting myself off towards the High Street, that this is where I live? *A trip around the world*, I thought. The phrase snagged in my mind. I wondered, if I were to photocopy a fifty-pound note—what fifty-pound note?—if I were to photocopy a fifty-pound note and cut it out and give it to the ten-pound-note man, would he get the joke and pretend to be pleased, or might he, in some strange way, actually *be* pleased?

I looked into Brown's Shoppe. This was going to be a stopping journey. In order to be able to keep going, I would have to stop on the way. Brown's Shoppe caused me to feel curious for a moment about whether or not Stella Ramble, back when she'd been in control of her faculties, had felt for stacking-crates anything like the contempt she'd professed to feel for folding furniture.

I went past The Admiral and turned right onto the High Street itself, past the betting shop, the bank, the Indian corner store that isn't on a corner, Margin's, Elaine's, Videosyncratic, A Cut Above, Shah's, The Hole in the Wall—I was slowing badly—the framer's. I stopped and counted to a hundred. In the window of the framing shop hung a sentimental pastel of a man rowing a girl on a lake: boating.

My piano-tuner grandfather wouldn't tell me jokes. He said I was too young and the only ones he could remember were 'royally filthy'. He died fast in hospital of pneumonia when I was seventeen, while I was in France. My mother phoned three days later and persuaded me not to come back. When I got home at the end of the summer, I asked her what she'd done about his things. I was thinking particularly of his piano, a plain, turn-of-the-century Bechstein upright. What I said was, 'What did you do about everything in his house?' And she replied, 'Oh, there wasn't really anything there.'

I set off again: motor parts, televisions, autumn bulbs, foil-effect bedheads, illegal axolotls, the smell of the Golden Fry, Renton's Copy Shop—again I had to pause. I leant into the recess made by the Renton's front window and tried to assume the undeceived stance of the little boy in Stella Ramble's hat-shop photograph. I thought I remembered that he'd had his hands in his shorts pockets, so I put my hands in my coat pockets where I found a small parcel. It had '*glass!!*' written on it. I didn't understand and pulled apart the wrapping. Johnson had given me his jade necklace.

I hadn't been going to the library, I hadn't been going anywhere, but when I was able to move again, that's where I went, muddling my way through the heavy entrance doors. I couldn't think what else to do.

I wasn't signed in on a computer, but one of the machines was free. Good enough: I sat down and began to use it.

First I looked up 'aftermath'. From the mid-sixteenth century it meant a year's second crop of grass, or 'aftermowth'—nobody hoovering their lawns back then. About a hundred years later, the word acquired the meaning it has for us now, i.e. in 1724, 'aftermath' did mean, as we now know it, aftermath.

I can't even imagine the full extent of Johnson's vocabulary, but 'maximagantic' doesn't formally exist. I found this out and then moved on to pigeons. The most noticeable problem for pigeons isn't paratyphoid, but missing toes. How many feral pigeons have the standard-issue number of toes? Bumble foot, per se, is unrelated to this question. Bumble foot is an infected wart. What I wanted to know was the reason for so many pigeons being stumpy, and the answers I discovered were these: if they stand in lime, or in their own gangrene-infected droppings, or if their feet become snaggled in the sort of human detritus that cuts off the blood supply, the toes will rot away. This tended to explain my erratically milling pigeons.

I returned to words. I felt convinced there had been one in particular I'd wanted to check, and it was with a small sense of triumph that I remembered I'd been asking myself about the noun 'squeeze', as meaning 'cast' or 'mould'.

I think I'd expected this to be a mid to late twentieth-century slang term, but it went back to the archaeologists of the 1850s. Engagingly, to me, Victorian burglars had used it this way as well. For example, a Victorian burglar might carry a lump of wax to take a 'squeeze' of a key. From what I could tell, the epigraphers had got the term into print first; but that settled nothing about who had pinched the usage from whom, supposing it wasn't a case of convergent evolution.

I felt much better now even than I had when I'd hit the outside air, *and* it came to me what 'a trip around the world' meant: not just me on the High Street, but also, in Bedford-speak, the extra-judicial beating of a police suspect in the back of a moving van.

As I wondered what to do, whether perhaps to shift to The Hole in the Wall, I was reminded of the thought Johnson had had in there—that those wild animal skins we consider the most glamorous are intended by their original owners to pass for river mud, gravel, dead grass and the like. If, I said to myself, you were a predator adapted to the roads that run laterally off the average English high street, what you'd want would be a coat that allowed you to blend in with the cracked paving stones and litter in the front area of a shabby Victorian terrace. Thus camouflaged, and hidden amongst discarded bicycles and rotten furniture, you could wait as long as it took for an infant to fall behind its nagging, shopping-laden mother. Then, simply, you'd pop up the steps, break the kid's neck, drag it back down with you and gorge yourself behind the bank of dustbins.

'No offence,' said a voice behind me, 'but are you using that computer?'

I hadn't been sitting long enough to recover much, and left the library with all the grace of a convict in a chain gang, shuffling blankly ahead—*ahead?*—until an elusive impulse made me backtrack and go into Renton's Copy Shop, '5p Each or £4 for 100'.

The usual Renton's man was behind the counter. I could hear that he was smiling as he said, with exaggerated woe, 'Cold, finally.'

'Yes, finally,' I said. 'But this is England after all.'

'Oh,' he said, 'you can't do much about it.'

I had a little change in my purse, still. I bought 500 sheets of 80g white A4, with the curious tag line on the packet, I read it twice, 'Internal Documents'.

'Hang on, let me get that door for you.'

Outside again, it occurred to me that I was on a course back to the flat. The thin dread I'd felt all week intensified sharply, and yet, when I reached the corner of my own street, I was disturbed by the certainty that I didn't have what it would take to make it all the way to my building. What had I been thinking of, going out after a fall, on painkillers, without crutches?

I don't know. I hadn't been thinking, is the answer.

Just past The Admiral I got completely stuck. That was it. I stood and marvelled at what an absurd kind of crisis this was. My building was right there, but I knew I couldn't make it that far, even to sit on the front wall.

I'd gone and forgotten to find out about 'gangbusters', scientific names for 'pond scum' and the origin of the ironing board. I should have made a list, I thought.

I thought about sitting down, down and out, right where I was on the pavement.

I counted to a hundred. Behind me, the door to The Admiral was open. There it was, The Admiral, darkly asthmatic; its carpet, sinking and blue. I'd never been in on my own before. So what?

With a horrible, shambolic gait, and swearing for solace, I made it up to the bar. I glowered at the last remains of my money. 'Pint of bitter,' I said. Only then did I notice that the place was devoid of customers.

The landlord, George, handed me my change. Now I really had nothing, or, to be precise, enough, but no more, for one phone call.

'You sit down, I'll bring it over,' he said. 'Put your shopping down.'

For some reason all the bar stools were against the far wall.

I tried to reply but my lips were trembling. *Thnks*, I said in my head. I gritted my teeth, held my breath, closed my eyes—pain: severe—Christ Almighty—then set off to sit at the table where I'd sat with Mrs Shaw.

He put my bag with the paper in it on her chair—'Internal Documents'? I looked inside and found that the back of the packet had a list on it of the various paper grades one could choose from: 'Internal', 'External', 'Presentation' and 'Prestige'. 'Internal Documents' was the cheapest and was only for black-and-white.

I tried not to think, as in: *Switch your brain off, Ramble*. End of story, right?

Hey, I thought, there's that girl with the gimpy legs mooching along the High Street, and—tell me she isn't handing *photocopied money* to a beggar?

Then again, there's this view that you should sort your head out a little bit previous, so they can't get you. *Thnks*.

'You all right over there?'

He was talking to me.

I looked down and saw that there was next to no drink left in my glass.

The bar stools were along the bar and several men were sitting on them. George, the landlord, turned on the television up above my head. What?

I laughed out loud.

Had he not so recently enquired, I think George might well at this point have asked me, was I all right?

Well I was. It had just struck me that the more I thought

about this plan of carrying on as though nothing had happened, the less I felt like doing it; and the reason I laughed out loud was that I'd been able to say to myself, in fact I did say to myself: girl, your meters are running backwards.

Also, I laughed because I was drunk. I found myself imagining Con jumping up out of his stupor, discovering that I wasn't back yet and coming down to the streets to find me. I pictured how he would step into the pub to ask whether anyone had seen me around—I'm noticeable, I don't take much describing—and how, there I'd be, mired and awkward, behind my empty glass.

But this was all wrong. He wasn't going to come and get me. He'd collapsed like this before, more than once. I knew very well he was going to be unconscious for hours. Once, he'd slept like this, dead to the world, for thirty-four hours.

No one was coming to get me.

What happens next? I finished off my beer and asked myself this question in words. Well, I'm going to *be smart—thnks*, I said to myself, I'm going to *be smart*.

It wasn't enough of an answer, and yet, as I thought it over, I found, at last, I found I knew—I quietly knew what it was I had really been waiting for. I was in it: next had begun. Next was now.

Why had I downed three coproxamol—three, plus a pint? Too late to worry. There will be gaps, I told myself, but you must hold steady. Alcohol, too, is a painkiller.

My mind wandered for a moment dangerously away; and then, with tipsy particularity, there I was explaining to myself what I needed to do.

First, I had to solicit one of the men at the bar to lend me his arm, just as far as my front door. If one of them would be a gent for a couple of hundred yards, I could surely do it. I was in England, in The Admiral, after all.

Surely all I had to do was ask. I closed my eyes but somebody barked and I slid back into focus.

Second, I needed to get up to the flat and print out my Internal Document.

A few days ago I was drifting past The Admiral when a man lurched towards me with a black-and-white photocopy of a ten-pound note.

Well, I wasn't about to leave it behind. I had ideas for what to do with all the talk from inside my head.

And I needed to get my favourite books, my crutches, clean knickers, the rest of the coproxamol, whatever I could fit in my messenger bag. I realised I'd already made a list for myself in case the flat burnt down. I'd got it worked out already: books, knickers, toothbrush, coproxamol. And money? Money for the night bus?

I leant back in my chair, sick at heart.

I felt sick and shut my eyes, ready to give up, except—except the answer was right there, waiting for the question.

A heady great wad of tenners would do it, and speed me on my way.

All I needed was a not-yet-paralytic gent from along the bar.

I sat forwards again, took a deep breath for courage, felt a little dizzy and put my head in my hands. *I think perhaps you dropped this egg.* Hey, I have to tell you this—!*bam!*—*expletive*—what the hell, right?—as one autistic vampire to another—*no offence.* I sat forwards and ended up with my head in my hands, but was buoyed by a picture that buoys me even now.

There's you, a bit dismal, getting from A to B on a night bus crowded with drunkards, though happily you've nabbed a seat by the window. And there's me. I'm the delinquent and bewildered creature who has nabbed the seat at your side. So the bus is speeding its way through the darkness when, to your dismay, as I picture it, you find me laying, in your lap, my head—shamelessly laying it in your lap, packed full of thoughts like a suitcase jam-packed with handkerchiefs. And at the exact weight of these thoughts—when your surprise at my impropriety has dwindled—you, I picture, all of an instant grasp that this insolently sleeping creature must be your friend, Ramble, whereupon you're supposed to say to yourself—this is how I see it: 'Can it be true? My friend Ramble? What an amazing piece of luck! When she wakes, by God, I'm going to tell her the very worst jokes I know and all my best stories!'

With this, I got myself upright. And I walked.